The WAR CANOE

The WAR CANOE

Jamie S. Bryson

Alaska Northwest Books®

Anchorage • Portland

Library of Congress Cataloging-in-Publication Data
Available upon request

Book compilation © MMVIII by
Alaska Northwest Books®, an imprint of
Graphic Arts Center Publishing Company
P.O. Box 10306, Portland, Oregon 97296-0306
503/226-2402; www.gacpc.com

Cover art © 2008 by Christine Cox

President: Charles M. Hopkins
General Manager: Douglas A. Pfeiffer
Associate Publisher, Alaska Northwest Books®: Sara Juday
Editorial Staff: Timothy W. Frew, Kathy Howard, Jean Bond-Slaughter
Production Coordinator: Vicki Knapton
Cover Design: Vicki Knapton
Interior Design: Alyson Hallberg

Printed in the United States of America by Lightning Source

To my mother, Elizabeth

Foreword

Southeastern Alaska is a long, narrow strip of land, water and islands called the Panhandle. It extends from the main body of Alaska south and east along the western edge of Canada. The only roads into Southeast terminate at Haines and Skagway at the north end, and Hyder at the south end. The five hundred miles between road heads is a mountainous, tree-covered archipelago containing the nation's largest national forest, the Tongass.

The Stikine River flows out of Canada and cuts the Alaska Panhandle in half at Wrangell, a small town on the north end of a forty-mile-long island also called Wrangell. It is the home of twenty-five hundred people and one of the oldest towns in Alaska.

The Tlingit Indians settled centuries ago at the mouth of a salmon stream thirteen miles down the island shore from what is now Wrangell. They traveled the Stikine River for trade and warfare. In 1834 the Russians selected a harbor at the north end of the island for Redoubt (Fort) Dionysius, built to control trade on the Stikine. In 1839 the Russians leased the fort to the British as a base for the Hudson's Bay Company, which was trading heavily with Indians, fur trappers and miners up the Stikine River in

Canada. The British called the redoubt Fort Stikine. The lease was in effect when the United States purchased Alaska in 1857. Americans changed the name to Fort Wrangel. The "Fort" was dropped when the U.S. withdrew its military garrison in 1888. Later, for some obscure reason, the second "l" was added to the name.

Tlingit Indians moved in around the fort early to trade with the military. Over the years, Indians have been the major part of the population, intermarrying with soldiers, trappers, miners and fishermen who settled in the community. In the early years of American settlement, Indians abandoned their Native ways at the urging of well-meaning Christian missionaries and adopted the ways of the new settlers.

After Alaska gained statehood, in 1959, the Indians in Wrangell, along with Native peoples throughout the new state, became aware of and concerned about the disappearance of their culture. Extensive efforts have been made during the last twenty-five years to preserve Indian culture and educate people about it.

Author Jamie Bryson published *The Wrangell Sentinel* during the 1970s, right after the Alaska Native Claims Settlement Act of 1971 passed Congress and further encouraged Alaska Natives to investigate and preserve their heritage.

Wrangell still is an isolated community at the mouth of the Stikine River, with no road connection to the mainland. It is served daily by jetliners and almost daily by state ferries. Cruise ships stop during the summer so visitors may view the totems and other signs of the Indian culture. Unlike other early Alaskan towns, the Indian culture is more dominant in Wrangell than that of the Russians, British or Americans. There are no Russian churches, as there are in Sitka, Kodiak and Kenai. There are no gold-rush relics, as there are in Skagway, Nome and Fairbanks. There are no monuments to Captain Cook, as in Anchorage. But there are totem poles and petroglyphs (early stone carvings).

Bryson's story, though fiction, is accurate in the awakening of Indians and non-Indians to the culture of the original settlers of the Wrangell area, whose huge dugout canoes sped the waterways of Southeast Alaska where modern diesel-driven state ferries now travel.

Although Bryson's book is written for youths, it has lessons for readers of all ages.

It's a unique story about a melding of cultures in a remote corner of the United States, a nation noted for the melding of diverse cultures from around the world.

Lew Williams, Jr.
Ketchikan Daily News

Preface

I first saw Wrangell and Wrangell Island in 1970, when I arrived to edit a community newspaper fallen on hard times indeed. *The Wrangell Sentinel* — now a thriving, fine little weekly newspaper — in the spring of that year was pretty well into its death throes, all of its fires out save one, you might say.

Like the Englishman "Editor" in this book, I found the premises dusty, forlorn, ill-lighted and all but abandoned, but with a certain spark that drew me into first editing and then owning the paper.

In the years I have called myself a Wrangellite, I also have come to love my town. It took me to its heart when I and my seven children — the youngest only two months old — were struggling to overcome our confusion and bitter shock and loneliness on the death of my wife, their mother, in an air crash in the summer of 1972. The town was so kind and supportive and utterly understanding that I have always felt I owed Wrangell a debt I could never fully repay.

I wrote this little book in honor of this joyous, energetic, obstinate, feisty little metropolis. The story was two years in the original writing. Most of it got onto paper aboard my thirty-foot sailboat while she lay in Shoemaker Bay marina at Wrangell from 1981 to 1982.

I hope my friends and neighbors in Wrangell like the book and find it factual and believable. If they don't, they'll sure let me know about it — small towns are like that, thank goodness.

I can't claim, as is the fashion, that all characters and incidents in the story are purely made up and bear no resemblance to real-life persons living or dead. Two characters are indeed taken from real life — Blackie and the trapper Hank Hudson.

Blackie was patterned after Eugene Zennie (Blackie) Madden, a good friend. In fact, Blackie was my first friend in Alaska and he stayed a solid one even though my citified ways sometimes made his brow furrow and brought a low growl of a "My, my" from him. He never let me down, ever, not once. He never let any of his friends down. Blackie's dead now but his shop is still there. I seldom pass it without thinking of him. Of course, all the incidents regarding Blackie in this book are made up. They didn't happen. I invented them. I like to think he'd approve.

Hank Hudson is patterned after the late Roy Allen, the trapper of Three-Way Pass at the south end of Etolin Island. Roy was smart and wise. He used to come out of the swirling snow some nights, into the newspaper office where I was burning the midnight oil, and have a chat. He was always welcome there. Roy was a true character and I always thought that if I ever got the time to write a book, he'd sure be in it — and he is. And I hope Roy would approve.

The historical facts about the naturalist John Muir are, as far as I could make them using the volumes available, accurate. The great Native leader Towaatt is portrayed accurately according to history. Towaatt's gravestone actually was found lying askew in the Native cemetery at Cemetery Point just south of town. I found the stone on a rainy afternoon in 1982 when I went for a stroll there, looking for a way out of an impasse in writing this story. Towaatt was already in the book; his gravestone was not. Imagine my surprise at finding it by chance like that. It sent me off to the library to find out more about him, then on a writing tear that lasted a week. It was very exciting. It was like meeting the venerable old Towaatt himself. I would hope that by now the stone has been taken over by the town museum, or at the very least has been set up in a place of honor at the cemetery. Towaatt was a hero who died for his people. Nobody seems to know where his grave actually is, but the evidence points to Shustak Point, across the bay from town.

Finally, the episode regarding the hanging of the Native Scutdoo was written by Mrs. Winnie Williams, a one-time co-publisher of *The Wrangell Sentinel*, from an interview with a Native who recounted the story from firsthand knowledge.

The rest of the characters and incidents in the book are made up, and if any of my friends and neighbors think they recognize themselves there, it is purely coincidental. This is a work of fiction built on a framework of historical fact.

J.B.

It was dawn in Alaska's Alexander Archipelago. A cold black night was beginning to give way to the first gray light of a new day. Emerging from the gloom were timbered islands with their rocky beaches, slate-colored sea and — off to the east — range after range of saw-toothed, snow-covered mainland mountains.

A pod of killer whales swept suddenly into the seawater channel bordering Wrangell Island's rugged eastern shore. The killers herded everything in their path northward. Seals — the lucky ones — slipped black and shiny onto chilled rocks, terror in their big, round eyes. Schools of fish made whirring sounds as they fanned the water's surface, skidding this way and that in panic.

In the depths of the ancient, deserted forests, crows and ravens began to call. They chattered, scolded, whistled and clicked and clucked in a raucous, echoing morning symphony.

From their special trees, eagles rose to meet the day. One began to circle silently in the frigid air above the waking town of Wrangell at the island's northern tip.

On Main Street, below, Blackie appeared from the close warmth of the cluttered apartment he shared with his wife above their rickety auto-repair garage and filling station. He peered over the unpainted rail of his sagging porch, noted the disreputable condition of the porch and the failing, paintless, century-old siding of the building — and was not disturbed by the ruin.

In fact, Blackie was elated this morning. He scratched himself liberally through his dirty union suit, stretched, took a long look at the waters and at the mountains and finally at the clear blue vault of the sky to be sure. Then he smiled a broad, toothless smile and called through the door to his wife: "Hey, y'all hustle out heah 'cuz I see sunshine a-comin'." Then to the morning itself Blackie called: "Hello deah mow-nun, hello deah sunshine," and he did a shuffly dance, shaking his porch alarmingly until his wife came out and made him stop.

Barely a hundred yards north of Blackie's place, in a green-painted frame house on Cow Alley, orphan Mickey Church woke face-down in his sagging bed. He lay, arms encircling his pillow, and listened for rain. He heard none. Mickey sat up, lifted a blind from his window, fisted off the dirty pane, saw blue sky with a trace of gold now to the east, and grinned.

The boy leaned far over and searched the dust under his bed, found an old shoe and drew it out. From deep in the toe he retrieved a crumpled package of cigarettes, lit up, and lay back blowing smoke at the peeling ceiling, feeling fine.

At *The Citizen*, Alaska's oldest weekly newspaper — and very near to being Alaska's smallest — Editor was out on the sidewalk squinting eastward from under his green eyeshade.

Editor was there early, or, more accurately, late, from working all night getting the week's *Citizen* finished.

Editor cast his weary gaze upward, saw an eagle swooping low and waved a greeting. He noted the sun's promise in gold against the pale blue sky behind the mountains and, like the boy and Blackie, smiled. He watched his eagle glide away. The bird passed over the sawmill, swooped low over the cannery, scattering gulls, and finally began circling over the harbor.

At the fishing boat float, Hank Hudson, just in from his camp at Spruce Pass, was fastening his outboard scow's painter to a rusty cleat amid a few how-dees and hullo Hanks from the waking line of boats. Followed closely by his wolflike dog, Hank began his coffee rounds of the fishing fleet. He was welcome on every single boat. Hank Hudson was a loved old man and he gloried in it. Still, there was a certain loneliness in him.

Editor's eagle, its harbor inspection complete, rolled gracefully to the level, flapped its long wings for speed, and continued out the two-lane highway to eventually begin lazily circling, again, at Five Mile. Below, on the beach next to the road, Tom Lincoln bent to his work willfully, his chain saw buzzing. Freshly cut, fragrant slices of firewood fell regularly at his feet. When the sun began to push past the tops of the mountains, sending pale yellow rays into the high valleys and causing the timber to shimmer, he shut down his saw and just watched.

Tom Lincoln welcomed the sun to the ancient land of his Tlingit forefathers, and when he could — or imagined he could — feel the warmth of the ascending orb, he said aloud, "Uncle would have smiled at this morning. He surely would have smiled."

Then the husky Native went back to work, his saw slicing slab after slab of newly cut spruce.

The soaring eagle was a speck from below. The bird cut the air with quick chops of its long wings, then began a graceful gliding, turning game. It moved its white head from side to side, studying the sky around and the land and water far below.

The bird sensed but did not note — for why should it? — the dark outline of a ship far off, approaching the island.

Finally, the eagle ceased its play, sped off eastward, and soon left the little pinpoint of civilization far behind.

At ten o'clock, the ship, which was the blue-and-gold-painted Alaska state ferry *Taku*, motored by the very last point of land blocking its direct passage to the Wrangell dock, and turned slowly townward.

At least one *Taku* passenger, Professor Waldo Bernet, felt keen elation as Wrangell hove into clear view. Set in a park of timber that shone and glistened, Wrangell belied its frontier robustness. Even its oldest and most sagging waterfront buildings looked plumb and square and new again from afar on this clear morning. Fishing boats rode the waters nearby; a tug on some important errand bustled away from the jetty, its stern buried in its own wake. Smoke rose from the sawmill and houses stair-stepped up the hills.

It all looked as he imagined — dreamed — it would. The professor actually stifled a sob. He had arrived. Dr. Waldo Bernet, social anthropology, history and English, reflected on how he had come so many thousands of miles to work and live in this remote outpost in the North.

As it happened, he was smitten with Alaska from afar. A short thesis as a history student was enough to do it. From that seed an interest grew and grew and finally Bernet was helplessly enmeshed. He found himself one day presenting his case before his dean, asking for a leave from his teaching post.

"Go," the dean had said, "because goodness knows you'll be no real use here until you do. Go, take notes and then come back to us."

An understanding sort of chap, the dean, Bernet had ruminated later. He had expected to be fired.

So it was that finally the professor, a thin, almost gaunt man with a high voice, long-fingered delicate scholar's hands and a love of his fellow man that amounted to fire in his soul, shouldered his duffel bag, grasped the handle of a battered suitcase and emerged from *Taku's* cavernous car deck to climb the ramp to the Wrangell shore.

When he had gained solid ground, the professor made his way to the little varnished wood terminal building and dropped his gear outside. Bernet stuck his head inside the building, extending his long neck, and looked around. A crowd of travelers and greeters and senders-off, all dressed in robust, practical, warm clothing, mostly of wool, milled about or lounged on benches. There was a hum of conversation and a lot of good-natured shouts and ribbing.

Slightly intimidated, Bernet began to back away, until he saw an old man looking straight his way with bright eyes. The first finger of the man's big hand was wagging at the professor. Bernet pointed at himself and the man nodded his head and smiled.

Bernet pushed through the crowd and the old man began to move toward the professor.

"Well," said the stranger when Bernet stood before him. "You got here. You made it."

"Indeed," replied Bernet. "Ah, I'm looking for Muir

Mountain." It was the first thought that came to the professor's mind. Besides, he *was* looking for the mountain. After actually arriving at Wrangell, seeing the famous mountain was the most important thing he hoped to accomplish today. Bernet caught himself. "Oh, you weren't perhaps sent here to meet me, were you?" he asked the old man.

"Well," the stranger replied, expelling a blue cloud of pipe smoke and pulling the ear of the knee-high dog that stood next to him. "In a manner of speaking I may have been sent here to meet you. But I wasn't . . ." He laughed, emitting more smoke.

"Oh," said Bernet. "Well, my, my."

"Never mind," said his companion. "Out the door with you, young fella. Turn right, look left — Muir Mountain. Except folks around here call it mostly Dewey Mountain. They don't know any better, see."

Bernet retreated to the door, found his gear, and started out. Ten minutes later he stood bareheaded in a puddled play yard at the foot of a little round-topped, spruce- and hemlock-covered mountain. It was the same hill naturalist John Muir described vividly in his writings. The professor was thrilled.

"Up there somewhere," he said aloud, cocking his head this way and that. His eyes searched the summit of the wooded hill.

"Yep," agreed a voice beside him. "Yep."

Bernet turned to find the old man from the ferry terminal, arms folded across his chest, accompanied by his wet wolf dog, taking in the view from the play yard, too.

"They named this little hill after Dewey — Spanish-American War or somesuch, see. Foolishness if you ask me. It's Muir Mountain plain and simple, it is. By golly, yes. John Muir, the great man hisself, lit a fire up there in eighteen hundred and seventy-nine and scared the firewater out of the Natives. That's a lot of bunk, actually, about the Natives being scared. They weren't fools and they'd seen plenty of fires. What scared them, if they were scared, they figured anyone would climb a mountain in a storm in the night and have a fire, well, that one maybe needed watching." The old man whirled a finger around an ear. "Maybe he was a little funny-like."

The professor studied the serious, weathered face of his companion. "Muir said he did it — lit the fire — to see how the trees behaved in a storm. It lit up the clouds and people down here couldn't tell just what it was. The clouds glowed from the fire," Bernet said. He stroked his pointed beard, staring intently at the old man.

"I understand that," thundered his companion. "Perfectly well. John Muir, a great man, real Alaskan even if he did come from Outside somewheres. He loved this country." He swept an arm around taking in the view of the straits, mountains and islands. "He took care of the country. He was strong in the woods. Talked to trees. I do that."

The old man blew a great cloud of smoke at the sky and suddenly extended a weathered hand. "Hudson," he said. "Hank Hudson. This is Chinook. Half wolf." He laid a hand on the dog, who wore a rope knotted around his neck, the frayed end trailing behind him. "Cops say he has to be leashed, so he drags that rope all over town."

Bernet held out his hand to Hank Hudson. "Bernet," he replied.

"Know it," said the old man, gripping the professor's hand. He put his left hand over the right and gazed into the educator's eyes.

"New teacher up at the high school, and good luck with it, Bernet. The kids need good teachers. You one? Good?"

"Yes," replied the professor simply.

"Thought so," said Hudson. "Minute I saw you I thought so. It's the eyes. I came down to the ferryboat to see you ashore, sort of check you out. Well, I have."

Hank Hudson laughed and roughed the dog's back with his hand. "I'm your first friend in Wrangell and I'm a good one to have. I love this country. So will you."

"Well," said the professor. He could add nothing.

"Exactly," replied Hank Hudson.

2

When Dr. Bernet seriously told his students he was taking them on a trip into the past right there in the classroom, they glanced furtively at one another and winked or laughed. Mickey Church did more — he smirked, right at the teacher, who smiled and started out:

". . . Noon, August of 1822. Baleful black eyes peered from a forest not far from Wrangell. A stone's throw away, a Russian brig slid along a rocky shore. The ship's heavy sails rumbled in a fitful breeze, barely pulling her along.

"The sailors guessed the Natives were hidden nearby, plotting murder and plunder, for these were dangerous waters. For days the armed brig had been working her way slowly and laboriously eastward into the heart of the archipelago. She sailed when there was wind and went under tow of her own boats when there was not. Earlier this day a picked group of the huskiest sailors had clambered over the ship's dark side into their longboat and towed her for five miles across a mirror-surfaced strait. Then this welcome zephyr had found them.

"The brig coasted in close to the last small island she would see before finally crossing to her destination and dropping anchor. The ship glided silently, leaving no wake. The grateful oarsmen lounged and joked on deck. They were resigned to pulling again when their commander, Lt. Dionysius Zarembo, bade them to. The sailors were inured to the dismal rain that had fallen unceasingly since the ship left Russian New Archangel.

"The river, or at least the cleavage through the mountains where the river came and met salt water, was in view straight ahead, now nine miles or so across the rippling water. The river was a powerful force, wide and fast and rich with game, fed by numerous glaciers. It was an important trading highway and it made the ship's destination important, too.

"Closer than the river entrance by a few watery miles was the long, mountainous island the ship sought. There the anchor would finally splash down. A fort would be built and trading begun. It was a dangerous business, but this new trading outpost was important in the Russian expansion of its Alaskan enterprise.

"Likely there would be deadly confrontations between the Russians, who would stay and build the fort, and the Natives whose village was, for all intents and purposes, being occupied by a foreign power. And few ships had ventured this deep into the land of the Tlingit. Those that did always seemed to find plenty of trouble.

"Lieutenant Zarembo said arrangements had been made with the Native chiefs for building the fort and that his little brig, named *Chichagof*, was proceeding with assent of the rulers of this brooding land.

"No Natives had been seen, but the air was heavy with foreboding. In fact, the Russian ship had seldom been without an escort, unseen, of war canoes that sped silently in her wake out of sight along shorelines. The canoes hid in bays while their crews scouted the brig from the trees and, in the night, the war canoes boldly closed the ship, seeking an opening to take her.

"Now, from the village on the northern shores of the big island the Russians sought, hundreds of pairs of eyes followed the brig's slow passage along the far shoreline. The sails showed as a light-colored blotch against the dark timber. The image grew and grew as the ship approached, and the excitement in the village intensified."

Bernet had become inflamed with the telling of his tale. He paced before his desk at the front of the old classroom. His students were silent now, intent.

"Soon now, a great moment in the history of South-eastern Alaska — of all Alaska — would take place," said the teacher.

"That brig would round into that bay entrance down there," he pointed out the high windows. "Her sails would be taken in, the anchor would be set and the commerce that would last for many decades and change the lives and destinies of the Stikine Tlingits forever, would begin."

To his surprise, this account of the arrival of the Russian ship put Mickey Church on the edge of his battered school-desk seat. As the skinny teacher droned on in his peculiar high voice about Natives and ships and furs and the tough Russians, who came to barter, or to fight if they had to, Mickey saw it all in his mind's eye. He envisioned the sailing ship rounding up ponderously near the shore in front of the village, her sails being bundled up, her anchor cable going out. Mickey could peer over a nearby windowsill and sight across Wrangell's rooftops to glimpse the water. Perhaps he could see the very spot where the ship anchored.

The teacher continued. He told of the building of the fort, the efforts of the Natives to displace the Russians there, the fear of the white man, alone in his stockade surrounded by hostile tribes. Mickey took it all in, despite his old disdain for school.

He stretched in his seat in an old habit of indifference, but immediately sat up again for fear his fidgeting might somehow distract Dr. Bernet from his story.

Finally the teacher broke off his lecture, straightened his already impeccably straight necktie, ran a hand over his thin but carefully combed hair and dropped a finger to his class seating chart. He leaned down to the names printed there and finally looked up and spoke in a thin, reedy voice that was nearly a squeak. And when he spoke, it was to Mickey.

"Mr., ahhhhhh, Church," Bernet said, staring across the high-windowed, oak-floored classroom at Mickey. There was a moment of silence interrupted only by several clunks and a hiss of steam from the heating radiator, then Bernet continued: "Mr. Church, what do you suppose the Tlingit people thought of that ship's coming? Remember, it was perhaps only the second or third ship the Natives had ever seen, and the only one with any intentions of putting white men ashore on a permanent basis.

"What do you — hmmmmmmm — think were their thoughts about this? Of the coming of the Russians with their ship and cannon and muskets and new ways?"

Mickey looked thoughtful, even startled. It had been a

long while since a teacher had called on him. A half-dozen terse and rude answers began to form, by habit, on Mickey's tongue, but faded as quickly. He stared at the teacher and Bernet stared back kindly, expectantly.

"Mr. Church," the teacher prompted, "the Russians came in that ship and put their men ashore, built their fort, put the Natives to gathering furs. It started a new phase in Tlingit history. There was cruelty and disease and liquor and murder, eventually, and the elders among the Tlingits, the thinkers, those with insight, surely sensed this coming.

"What do you suppose those elders were thinking as the *Chichagof* came closer and closer?"

Mickey stole a glance at Bugs Nielsen, who leered at him. Bugs expected fireworks.

Mickey turned to the teacher.

"I think," Mickey began, "that those elders were really worried. They were worried for their culture, ah, for their future, and they musta' been trying, ah, trying to plan how to sink that ship. Maybe they should have, too," he added defiantly.

"Exactly!" crowed the teacher. "Just what I myself think must have gone through the minds of the Native leaders. What to do about this? How to put this off, stave this off. The Russians were coming. It marked the beginning of the end of the Natives' sovereignty over this land. Already, in Sitka, where there was much strife between the races, much bloodshed, the story was clear — the Natives suffered whenever the white man showed up."

Bernet stared intently again at Mickey, letting a full half-minute tick away in silence.

"Ahhh, Mr. Church," the teacher finally said. "You yourself are Native, are you not?"

"Yes," replied Mickey Church loudly and sitting up straight at his desk for the first time anyone could remember, and running his eyes coolly over the class. "Yes, I am. I am Tlingit."

School over, Mickey and Bugs leaned against the building, waiting to stroll downtown. They watched the rain fold itself over the town and the bay and the strait beyond. It pelted the water, sent the building gutters running and left the timber on the hillsides dripping.

"Where did you get that from?" smirked Bugs. "What's this 'culture' and 'future' stuff?"

Mickey hunched into his wool jacket, crossed his rubber-booted feet, and slouched against the wall. He followed the flight of two ravens that sped past in the rain.

"Ah, I read about that somewhere. I know more than you think I do." Mickey rolled his eyes right, looking at Bugs without turning his head. "It's just a lot of bull," he added unconvincingly.

"Where do you think that ship anchored down there?" he asked Bugs, craning his neck to see the harbor.

Bugs spun around and looked closely at his friend, then laughed. "Nuts," Bugs said, spitting at the ground. "Mickey, you're nuts."

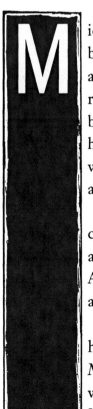

3

Mickey Church was orphaned as a baby. His mother became ill and died and his father was killed shortly afterward in a logging accident on Deer Island. He remembered neither of them. Mickey was taken in by a widowed aunt. She wasn't rich. Her old board house on Cow Alley had seen better days. But she was kind. He had a home and he was fed and clothed and, yes, even loved.

His aunt tried but she worked at the cannery days in the summer and drove a school bus all winter. She was awfully tired a lot of the time. And besides, boys — especially Mickey — could be a handful.

He liked to think of himself as orphaned, handicapped. The idea appealed to him — poor Mickey, lost his mother and father. No wonder he was so tough. No wonder he was going wrong. Mickey was experimenting with alcohol. He'd even been drunk a couple of times. He was building up a good store of cuss words. He smoked, hanging a cigarette from the corner of his mouth when he talked to other boys. He'd practiced that one in front of the mirror.

In his aunt's house he tried to behave. After all, it *was* her house. He didn't see any reason to hurt her feelings. It made him feel remorseful when she'd look at him sometimes with misty eyes, shake her head slowly, and then turn away.

So the day he got caught smoking marijuana he was more concerned about how she would take it than he was about himself — but only slightly more.

It happened on a Saturday morning. Wrangell was bustling. Main Street was crowded with pedestrians and cars and muddy pick-up trucks. Police Chief Jim Davis, alone in his second-floor office over the Elks Club, had arranged his lanky six-foot-five frame deep into a tilted chair in front of his window, and was taking it all in. A mug of steaming coffee stood within reach. So did a neatly stacked half-dozen oatmeal cookies, his breakfast. Davis sipped, munched and looked outside at one of God's rare gifts to this part of Alaska — another sunny day.

The policeman's view took in the street below, and on raising his eyes slightly, the colorful nest of frame houses on the lower skirts of wooded Muir Mountain. Of the mountain itself the chief had, by lowering his head slightly and looking up, almost the entire view.

Davis squinted and bracketed the historic hill in the window. He moved his head this way and that until he was pleased with the composition — window frame, trees, houses and the loom of the mountain. The balance fed some inner need in Chief Davis. He was an orderly man and took pleasure, this morning, in the fact that an orderly mountain arranged itself in an orderly manner in his window.

The chief was more or less hypnotized by the tableau and was beginning to doze when a brief flash of color in the trees near the mountain's round peak somehow got between his drooping eyelids and sped its message to his policeman's brain. His eyes snapped wide open and focused on the spot. There was nothing. With the patience borne of his breed he stared, intent, like a cat at a mouse hole. One minute passed, then two minutes, three. At five minutes, he was rewarded. He saw it again.

Chief Davis grunted and carefully and slowly began to unwind himself. Finally he stood, stretched, and fetched his binoculars. He rested the instrument on the windowsill, whirled the focusing wheel, found his target and said, "Yep, I thought as much."

The policeman put the binoculars away carefully, shrugged into his uniform jacket with the big gold badge that said CHIEF in black enamel lettering under which was the badge number, ONE, also in black enamel. He stood before the mirror and smoothed his jacket, gave the badge a swipe with a jacket cuff and put his hat on, adjusting it just so. He took a last sip of coffee, scooped up two cookies to take along, and let himself out of the office.

The chief strode purposefully across Main Street in the sunshine, said hello to Editor, who was out in his green eyeshade for a stretch, and headed up the side street that led to Muir Mountain. He cut between Irma Smith's cabin and the big house of the town druggist, and finally gained the path that would take him up.

Following a well-worn trail into the timber, Chief Davis soon found himself in the quiet and cool world of the Southeast Alaska rain forest. He took the path like a mountain goat, eating it up with ever-widening strides.

The chief was at full speed when he won the top and sailed into a clearing just as Mickey Church took a long, smiling drag on a strange-looking cigarette. Three other boys looked on in admiration. Mickey saw the police chief, palmed the sorry-looking weed into the dirt beside him, and allowed, with smoke still trailing out of his mouth and nose with the words, that he and his friends were enjoying the sunny day and the view and wasn't it pretty, Sir?

Chief Davis shook his big head sadly, motioned for the boys to rise, and marched them single-file back down the steep trail, across Main Street, up the covered ramp to police headquarters and into the office. He sat them down, found his cold coffee, sipped at it, grimaced, and got out some forms of paper. Humming tunelessly, the chief spread the papers ceremoniously across his desk and studied them.

The teenagers, who so recently had considered themselves alone and hidden in the forest, looked at the policeman balefully.

The mountain, thought Mickey Church, planning ahead as usual, just wouldn't do. And how did the cop know we were up there?

"Well," Chief Davis said, looking straight at Mickey from under furrowed brows, "nobody told me, that's for sure." The policeman had an annoying way of answering unspoken questions. It was one of his great strengths as an interrogator. One might say he could read minds. It sometimes seemed like it.

Mickey stared at the policeman, thinking fast and coming up with nothing.

Chief Davis said no more for the present, just eyed Mickey and his friends sadly. Time stretched out and the boys began to fidget. Mickey decided suddenly: We're going to jail, that's all. He's going to put us away. The policeman had spread the remains of the cigarette onto a shiny square of white paper. Mickey eyed the evidence with distaste and the beginnings of fear.

The chief let it go on for an agonizingly long time, then strode close to the boys, bent down and said, "Now, I'm going to let you young lawbreakers in on a secret. I have a very sensitive nose."

Mickey turned his head slowly and saw Muir Mountain through the policeman's window. He also saw the flags at the post office fluttering in a breeze that blew from the mountain toward the window. He saw, in his mind's eye, Chief Davis's nose, grown to enormous proportions, twitching, and he saw binoculars going up past that nose. Mickey paled.

"Yep," said Chief Davis in that annoying way. "Smelled it."

Then, it being a day with sunshine — a special thing — he did a special thing. "Get out of here," he snapped. "Scoot. Vah-moose. Don't smoke, don't chew, don't drink, don't do anything illegal, see? Go."

The boys flew away from police headquarters. The chief, back in his chair, watched them disappear down Main Street in the direction of the harbor, and smiled.

Word flashed through the ranks of the town's party-time youth, just as Davis knew it would.

Chief Davis became known as the cop who could smell pot at a mile. As he knew he would.

And his mystique grew a little more. Just as he expected it would.

4

It was shortly after this that Blackie found himself suddenly in trouble with the law. Not in trouble with Chief Davis, who liked and understood the grimy garageman, but with a visiting state trooper.

The trooper, who served Wrangell on a circuit basis, did not like Blackie on principle. To him, Blackie, with his grease-stained overalls, his beady eyes, cluttered garage and impudent way of somehow having his back turned whenever the trooper came near him, was a suspicious character. The trooper was almost sure Blackie had a criminal record.

Chief Davis was all the way sure Blackie had a record. He had checked it all out long ago, read the reports, shook his head, grinned and forgotten all about it. Blackie was a curious breed of man, a Cajun. Davis had known a few of the type — Louisianans descended from tough French settlers — and he understood them. The trooper did not.

The stage was set for an incident. And an incident with Blackie could be fraught with peril.

Blackie's place was housed in an ancient, sagging, rain-soaked building on stilts over the beach on the sea side of Main Street. All but the street entrance to the structure had been standing on its tree-trunk legs since well before the turn of the century. It was a narrow cavern of a place with a row of mud-and-grease-streaked windows running along the south side. The pilings were sinking into the bay mud, which gave the splintery floor an undulating character not unlike the surface of the sea. Blackie didn't spare any time for worrying about the supports. He figured they had over the years sunk as far as they were going to, and he was correct — they had done sinking and now were trying to return to dust. Rot was everywhere in the building's underpinnings. But the structure stayed, seemingly by force of habit, glued to Main Street, its body extended over the bay mud, buzzing six days of the week with the business of filling the gas tanks of cars and trucks and, when necessary, repairing their internal workings.

On the street in front were the two gas pumps, leaning drunkenly toward each other. Cars and trucks pulled in going either direction for refills. Blackie or his wife, a happy Tlingit woman, would saunter out in the rain to pump gas and to visit.

The station's office was chaos. Like the workshop behind it and the show window in front, it was the resting place for an assortment of items not necessarily of value in a garage business. The vertical tail from a crashed Cessna 170 airplane hung on a wall. Old clothes, magazines, empty cardboard boxes, rubber boots and fishing rods shared their places out of the rain with batteries, filters, lamps, cases of antifreeze bought at summer discount and stored against the fall rush, fan belts and more.

A counter extended three-quarters of the way across the office and behind that was an old wooden cable spool, rescued from the dump, which served as the office checker table. By the hour Blackie and his cronies clicked checkers there while they told stories and downed beers and sodas. In between, Blackie gassed the cars and sometimes adjourned to the dark shop to find the requisite tools and repair a car or two. While he worked back there, Blackie talked to his beloved building as the patriarch's skeleton cracked and groaned. "Ah know, ah know," he'd croon. "Your old bones is a' achin', just like old Blackie's, mmmm, mmmm, yes."

Blackie was a strange, lovable, tough, dumb-smart Louisiana man who hadn't always lived thus. But, come to think of it, taking everything into consideration, pretty much thus.

He left the South as a boy when he lied about his age to go to World War II. His specialty became jumping from airplanes by parachute, slung like a pack mule with guns and bombs and knives. Sometimes Blackie could be coaxed into telling blood-curdling stories of war that no one — knowing Blackie — doubted were true.

Blackie was not liked by everybody in town, but anyone who wanted to be Blackie's friend could be — Native kids, white kids, drunks, millworkers, mayors, editors, fishermen, crab-pot thieves, passing dogs, even policemen. Blackie wasn't choosy, but he was demanding. If a man crossed Blackie just once, then — bless his soul — he'd be Blackie's enemy. And that was bad.

The trooper fell into the latter category, much to his eternal regret, one rainy day in early October.

The lawman slammed into Blackie's and dropped a quarter on the counter. "Coke," he said, smiling tightly. "How's things, Blackie?"

"Ohhhh, now," Blackie drawled, looking up from a checker game with a friend. "Can't complain none. He'p yoself to the Coke. Cops is free 'roun heah."

The trooper left the quarter on the counter. "Who's winning?" he asked, popping the cap off his soda and tilting the bottle carefully to his mouth.

"He is," Blackie said, pointing to a fisherman as grimy, in his way, as Blackie. "Fact Jim's done won. Fact is, we ain't been too serious about this-here game — I got a car to fix and Jim's cuttin' wood out to his place. We been wastin' time." Blackie's finely tuned alarm system was flashing red lights. He wished the cop would drink his soda and leave.

But when they were alone, the trooper said, "Blackie, I hear you have a nice Luger pistol here. I'm really interested in World War II handguns. Do you think I could see it?"

Blackie's eyebrows rose in pleasure. "Say," he said, his alarm lights blinking out one by one, "I took that-there gun off a German sodjer in France. He didn't have no more use for it. He and me chased each other around in this-here ditch until he got shot — my, it was excitin'."

Blackie ducked out the door into the cold day, climbed the steps to his apartment, and returned with a murderous-looking black automatic. He pulled the trigger and the gun gave a clicking sound.

"Don't worry none," Blackie told the lawman, as he handed the gun over. "It ain't loaded."

"Hmmmm," the trooper mused, turning the automatic over and over in his hands, hefting it, aiming it at the center of the Cessna tail. Then he handed the gun back and hurried from the building, striding purposefully off toward the north.

Blackie's dark face clouded and he leaned outside to

watch the trooper in retreat. The lawman was headed straight toward the police station.

Across the street, Blackie spied Mickey Church lounging in the cold against a building, smirking at passersby and spitting now and then into the slush-filled gutter. Blackie motioned Mickey across.

"Hi, Blackie," the boy said. "You want me to . . . ?" Mickey motioned in the direction the trooper had gone.

"Yep," said Blackie.

Mickey took off after the officer. Ten minutes later he was back. "He's up at Chief Davis's pounding on the teletype," he said. "I looked through a window."

"Uh-huh," grunted the garageman, who stared at nothing, then said: "Mickey, go up to the phone across from the police station and watch. When he starts back here, y'all call me, quick."

Mickey was off again.

Blackie went to the back of his shop and readied some equipment. He placed his beloved Luger on the workbench and spoke to it. "I shore hate to do this, gun."

Fifteen minutes later the phone rang.

When the trooper burst into the office, Blackie was where he had left him, and the Luger was still on the counter.

"Okay," said the lawman, coming right to the point. "I thought so, Blackie. You're a felon in possession of a handgun. Sorry, but you'll have to hand it over. Then we talk charges. I got you."

Blackie shot the trooper a pained look. He picked up his Luger with a gloved hand and dropped it into the officer's out-stretched hand. There was a sizzling sound and a bellow of pain. The gun clattered to the board floor.

"Goodness," drawled Blackie. "I guess I left the gun on that-there stove by accident. Moved it just afore you came in but didn't notice she was hot 'cuz I had this-here glove on from some work I was a-doin' out back. Real important work. A accident."

The trooper, his burned hand thrust into the ice water in Blackie's old-fashioned soft-drink cooler, eyed Blackie ominously. "You danged well did that on purpose," he shouted. "You burned me and I'm going to arrest you, Blackie, for being a felon in possession of a handgun AND for assaulting an officer."

"Accident," Blackie repeated carefully. Then he dropped his bombshell. "Besides, the gun's a dummy. Firin' pin's welded. Been welded for — les' see now — been welded fer twenty-five, thirty years, yes sir. Can't shoot. It's a dad-gummed toy gun."

The lawman's eyes widened. He swished his hand around in the cooler. "Why, I heard it click when you pulled the trigger."

"Didn't neither," said Blackie. "Probably the floor. It's always making noises. And YOU never pulled the trigger, just aimed the gun at all my junk in here." He looked at the trooper innocently. "Ain't that right?"

The lawman left for a drive up the hill to the hospital to have his hand looked after, promising Blackie he would return. He didn't. The pin *was* welded. The stove *was* going, and Blackie *was* wearing a glove. And, well, it was better dropped.

After that Blackie didn't even bother to turn his back when he encountered the trooper. He just looked right through him. Besides that, he gave the lawman a nickname that the town loved and used and that the trooper grew to hate — Dudley Doright. And Blackie contrived in various other ways over the weeks and months to cause the lawman distress whenever his duties called him to Wrangell. All in all, the trooper lived to be sorry he'd ever tangled with Blackie, ex-felon.

"You really a criminal?" asked Mickey of Blackie.

"Cop made me ruin my German gun," Blackie lamented, ignoring the question and looking sadly at the Luger. "Took it off that-there German fella in France and kep' it nice all these years. Now it's ruint."

"You really a — ah — a felon?" Mickey persisted.

"Reckon so," Blackie conceded.

"What did you do?" Mickey was impressed.

"Ah, it was a long time ago," said Blackie.

"Tell me."

"Beat up a feller."

"Yeah? Did he deserve it?"

"Well," said the garageman. "I reckon he deserved it some. Not as much as I give him, mebbe."

"Did you really take that gun off a German, Blackie?"

Blackie stared at the boy. "You doubt'n my word, chile?"

Mickey shook his head quickly.

"Okay," said the garageman, picking up the Luger and sighting it in on the airplane tail. "He was a German sodjer a-tryin' to kill me.

"Which only goes to prove, Mickey, that you cain't trust no one in uniform. Then or now. Remember that-there."

5

It was the first time anyone could recall Mickey Church as anything but trouble in school. It was the first time anyone could recall Mickey Church studying. But Dr. Bernet was having a strange effect on Mickey and it brought about both those turnarounds in the boy.

In fact, Dr. Bernet was having that effect on a number of students. Strange as the teacher appeared with his intense and direct way and his outlandishly — for Wrangell — formal dress, he was becoming popular. The man knew each of his students by name and addressed them in the hallways with great energy and with an affection that they sensed accurately as genuine. He called out loud and squeaky greetings to them on the street and they responded cheerfully. It was going very well for Dr. Bernet.

The students were deep into the study of Tlingit culture. It was a revelation to most of them that they lived in a town so rich in history, the very town they always had thought of as plain, dull and ill-begotten.

Dr. Bernet traced the Ice Age and how it had fashioned the land and seaways between. He spoke of the Tlingits with such feeling and intensity and from such an obvious depth of knowledge that Mickey found himself electrified. So much so that in search of more about his past he stepped for the first time across the threshold of the city library.

When Mickey shyly approached the desk and addressed Mrs. Preston, saying almost in a whisper, "I want a book on Tlingits," the librarian, a loving, gray-haired old soul and a keen observer of Wrangell's young people, knew exactly how to handle the situation.

As if Mickey were a regular, she said in a friendly but professional tone: "Good afternoon, Mickey. You've timed it just right, you know. We have a new book in."

The librarian took Mickey to the shelf, talking softly to herself along the way as she gave the boy a subtle lesson in book-finding. She read off the authors. Said, "Let's see — A, B, C, D, — ahhh! We've found it," and pulled out the book. At the desk she quickly typed up a library card for the boy, handed it to him, stamped his book and handed him that and turned to another patron.

Mickey proudly carried his volume to a table and began to read. Later, with the book tucked securely under his arm, he left the building, but soon had it open again, reading as he walked along Main Street, where he collided with Tim Sipe. And that meant trouble.

"Say there, Indian," said Tim, the mill foreman's son, a bully of sparse and cruel intellect, "watch where you're walking, you jerk." And with that pronouncement, he shoved Mickey off the sidewalk into the water-filled gutter. The library book slipped to the wet walkway, its binding plastered to the concrete and its pages fluttering. The bully walked on, giving the book a vicious kick, which sent it skittering.

Mickey felt red rage. He lunged after Tim, caught the bigger boy, and unleashed a heavy clout to Tim's shoulder, spinning him around. Astonished, Tim grasped Mickey by his jacket lapels and hurled him against the door of the hardware store, then hunched to punch. The hardware store door opened at that moment and Andy Grimsby, all three hundred pounds of him, filled it. Grimsby raised an index finger high and waved it meaningfully at Tim. The boy spat out a curse, lowered his threatening right fist from under Mickey's nose, and stalked away down the street.

"Thank you, Mr. Grimsby," said Mickey.

"For nothing," chuckled the big man. "I was only trying to protect Tim." The hardware-store man laughed again from deep down inside his ample frame and backed inside, pushing the heavy door shut after him. A shaken Mickey picked up his book, carefully brushed the water and dirt from it, and continued on course.

■ ■ ■

As he neared the shore where a coarse gravel beach backed by high grass and timber awaited, Mickey closed the gas valve and the big outboard motor choked and died. The rooster tail behind his aluminum scow collapsed, fell upon itself, and humped into a wave that chased the scow down, lifted the stern gently, and passed underneath to break in a foam on the beach.

It was a misty morning but the skies above were clear,

promising that the sun ascending over the mountains of the island would bring at least a measure of warmth soon. The surface of the strait was leaden and flat and seabirds circled and dived there. Crows and ravens called from the land. The water beneath the flat-bottomed scow chuckled as the boat coasted in. The rough beach led to a grass-covered stretch between gravel and the timber. This was Old Town. Here Mickey's ancestors had once lived.

Mickey thrust an oar over the scow's stern and guided the craft in between rows of heavy stones arranged like shoreline ferry landings. There were other such rows. These and a few stumps, which had been totem poles, and some mounds of earth where buildings or fires might have been, were all that remained to show that once this was a busy place. The hand-hewn Tlingit canoes made of massive cedar and spruce logs had once lain in grandeur between the rows of rocks.

Mickey felt at ease running his own boat into this spot and securing it between these ancient and revered stones carried here by Tlingits like himself.

The boy toured the little village site, moving slowly, thoughtfully. He felt detached and strange. He felt secure. Here the incident with Tim Sipe was all but forgotten; it paled in this ancient, important place.

Mickey removed his wool jacket and shirt, ignoring the sharp chill of the morning. He pulled off his boots, rolled his trouser cuffs and walked into the ice-cold sea. His legs hurt at once, the water sending up waves of pain. He reached down and took hand-cups of seawater and threw it onto his head and back, making himself smile through it. Youths in past years came to the sea to toughen themselves for battle and for the hunt. They would plunge into the straits and when they could no longer stand the numbing cold, they would stand on the rock and gravel beaches naked and beat one another with sticks.

Mickey retreated finally to the grass and sat shivering there, seeing in his mind's eye a dozen boys like himself, naked and plunging into the sea. It had obviously happened like that, and right here at this place.

He leaned against a log, beginning to warm up. The presence of all who had lived and labored and died here was a fact to Mickey. They were here. Their spirits were around him, but he did not feel frightened or threatened. Quite the opposite, he felt welcome; the ghosts were at ease with their reposing young visitor. The sun climbed at last from behind the peaks and its pale light spread over the ancient land. Mickey's eyelids fluttered and he dozed.

He opened his eyes sleepily, squinted along the shore and saw movement — a dim, dark something was against the beach. He stared hard as the shape grew in size. When it finally came into focus, Mickey gasped.

A dark Tlingit war canoe sped silently along the shore. Its more than twenty paddlers stroked in a strong, easy rhythm. The craft had a haughty thrust-out bow and was elaborately decorated with carved, bold white swirls along its sides. Enormous painted-on eyes glowered just back of the sharp, high stem.

It came on, close against the beach, moving very fast and growing quickly ever larger. Mickey could see now that one occupant of the craft was not paddling. He was a swart, flat-faced individual wearing a funnel-shaped hat, a blanket robe, highly decorated, thrown regally across his broad shoulders. He occupied the high bow of the canoe, sitting well above his companions. He stared straight ahead. The paddlers bent to their work, each making a silvery swirl to mark the place where his paddle punched the cold morning sea. Here was a breathtakingly beautiful, haunting sight.

The canoe closed the point where the boy sat wide-eyed and barely breathing. The man in the bow barked something in a guttural sing-song voice and his companions briskly shipped their paddles. The canoe glided soundlessly in the morning stillness, losing weigh, and stopped, rolling gently opposite Mickey. The canoe's paddlers, their naked torsos and muscular arms glistening, sat rigid, staring ahead.

The man in the bow did the same, but finally swung slowly and stared at the boy across the water. Mickey gazed back unafraid. The boy felt a great pride in his past and in these men who reigned supreme in this land once and whose spirits reigned supreme still — forever.

That was all. The paddlers took up the rhythm once more and the canoe moved off, picking up speed quickly. It finally disappeared around a rocky point and did not reappear.

It was a dream. Mickey assured himself that it was a dream as he pushed his scow into the strait and shakily started the motor.

But it seemed real, and the impact was real enough. Mickey saw the canoe in his mind still and he saw the men. And the germ of an idea was planted that day. It grew and gripped the boy Mickey Church so firmly that it changed his life and assured his future, and through the years touched many and made their lives richer, too.

6

"W eel," drawled Blackie, tugging with grease-blackened fingers at the bill of his cap. "I reckon it could be done, Mickey. Sure it could, but it would take some doin'."

Mickey reposed in a checker-playing chair, his heels resting on the edge of the stove. His library book was propped in his lap, open to a picture of a Tlingit canoe in full race along a misty, timbered shore.

"Where do you reckon you could build it?" asked Blackie.

Mickey looked innocently at Blackie and gestured with a wave at the crookedly hanging door that separated the office from the dank, cavernous shop beyond. "Actually," he said, "I was sort of thinking . . ."

Blackie stroked his bristled chin. He peered at Mickey with his close-set eyes from under dark brows. Blackie was in deep thought and when

Blackie thought — it could be awesome.

Blackie came out of his reverie. "I know where we can git the log," he said. "It's a-gonna have to be a big 'un."

"Yipes," Mickey cried, jumping up and running past Blackie into the shop. Mickey measured off the length of the old building's interior with careful steps along the damp, sagging, timeworn planking. He found there was forty-five feet of work space, provided Blackie was willing to remove a ton of rusty, greasy junk and an old Ford station wagon — and if a falling-down, roofless rear porch might somehow be used.

Blackie snorted at the idea of removing the car, which rested on tireless wheels and was piled high with old parts and other miscellaneous junk.

"I was gonna fix that car up," Blackie said, pulling a face. "It's a good one."

"Yeah," said Mickey, peering through a broken window at the torn and junk-jammed interior. "Sure."

"May as well haul her out of here, if you say so," Blackie conceded, giving the boy a wink. "Probably be ten years 'fore I get to her anyway."

Blackie finally led the way back to the office. "Now, let's look at that-there picture in the book," he said, and they opened up the volume again. "My, myeeee — ain't that a purty boat. Lookie at that thingamajigger on the front-end. Now, that's a-gonna take some doin' to carve that out."

∎ ∎ ∎

Bill the Blowdown King was a tree-faller-turned-boss. That meant he had his own logging show. But it was a gypo outfit. That is, it wasn't much of one.

Bill was a tough little man whose people some time back came from Ireland to America and built railroads. Bill's grandfather drifted to Oregon and Bill's father drifted to Alaska and Bill hadn't drifted anywhere. He was part of the land. A small, sinewy, dark, crinkly-faced, bright-eyed man, Bill had left the surety of working for someone else felling trees to become a blowdown logger. Bill was sort of a logging clean-up man, taking on the always chancy and always frustrating and dangerous work of cleaning out areas of timber flattened by high winter winds. He liked his work, though. Currently, he and his partner, a bearded, silent giant gargoyle named Simon, were laboring on an unlikely lee shore twenty miles from Wrangell on Clarence Strait, getting together a log raft of blown-down hemlock and spruce. The work was done with a worn-out tractor of uncertain vintage, muscle-power, and just plain meanness. The logs were high in the hills that rose wet and swampy from a windblown, rocky beach on whose shore clung Bill's one-trailer (sleeping), one-shack (cooking and tool-storage) camp.

"We get this raft in the water," he told Simon cheerfully as the two stood in their tin hats, soaked with rain, on the beach beside their smoking, complaining Caterpillar, "and we'll go to town and have a party."

Bill figured the raft would fetch ten thousand dollars, enough to pay off all his bills for the season, repair the tractor for next year and finance at least part of a winter of revelry. He calculated that according to the regular routine of his life he would party for half the winter and spend the other half in jail.

"We get this raft behind the tug in, say, a week," he told Simon, "then we close this place up for the winter before the first snow gets here. We collect our money, we pay the bills, and we spend the rest on you-know-what — fun."

Simon smiled a slow smile, his lips bright red and moist behind his jet-black beard. His eyes twinkled.

Suddenly a blue Cessna 185 floatplane roared over the beach. It was Elwood Waters, Wrangell's number-one bush pilot, with the regular weekly grocery delivery. Bill and Simon rushed to the shore and pushed their rust-bucket of an iron workboat into the chilly sea. Bill jerked the outboard motor into wheezing, then roaring life and the boat began to make its way through outlying rocks and reefs toward the airplane, which had alighted on the water and was bobbing quietly half a mile from shore.

The little pilot had strict orders never to venture with an airplane anywhere near Bill's beach, no matter how much the logger tried to talk him into doing it. No one — not even Bill — knew where all the rocks were.

"And rocks," Elwood's boss had said with great seriousness, "sink airplanes, Elwood."

The boss had wrinkled his face into a terrible pucker and placed it very close to Elwood's face and added: "Bill will always try to get you to taxi the airplane to the beach. He will not try to get you to do that sometimes, Elwood. He will try to get you to do that every time. Don't do it, or you're fired!"

The warning had the ring of steel to it. Elwood figured his boss meant it. It had, however, come too late by several weeks. Elwood had been enticed toward the beach by the tough little Irish logger and by some miracle Elwood and the boss's airplane escaped unscathed.

Bill had arrived beside the bobbing Cessna without Simon. "He's up in the woods, can't come." The logger had shaken his head sadly and looked at the boxes and bags filling the Cessna's little cabin. "We'll have to get these supplies into the boat ourselves, Elwood. Lot of work. Unless," added the gypo-logger, "you wanna come to the beach. I'll guide ya. Know these waters like the back of my own hand. Besides, breakfast's on. Got fresh eggs, grits, steaks, hot coffee. *Doughnuts*."

With Bill driving the outrageous iron boat and Elwood following in the Cessna, they made their way shoreward.

The iron boat was making speed, pushing a creamy wave before its blunt and rusty bow and trailing a nice little rooster tail. Elwood, his hand on the throttle, toes perched on the rudder pedals gingerly, and his heart in his mouth, followed along at about fifty yards, also cutting a rooster tail. Just as it seemed they would make it nicely, the iron boat reared like a harpooned whale, jerked violently around, and stopped short. Bill, who had been standing grandly at the tiller, was levitated. He sailed majestically out of the boat in a perfect arm-and-leg-waving arc and crashed in a frothy splash into the sea.

Elwood's eyes widened, an "Oh gosh!" exploded from him, and a booted left toe mashed a rudder pedal to the cockpit firewall, while the throttle went in in short bursts. The Cessna responded, turning sluggishly at first for the open sea. How close to the rocks he came Elwood couldn't tell, but it was close. Finally, the airplane was pointed seaward and Elwood jammed the throttle in to the stop. The engine roared, the prop bit the air viciously with a loud wail and the plane, skittering from wave to wave, made for safety offshore.

Half a mile away Elwood finally killed the engine and the airplane came to a bobbing, dripping stop. The little pilot, breathing heavily, opened the cockpit door so the cool air bathed him. He lay back in the seat, eyes closed, saying over and over again: "Thank you, Lord, thank you, Lord."

Eventually a sopping, grinning, thoroughly unperturbed

Bill arrived. "That's one I didn't know about," he called from the iron boat. "I reckon I know 'em all now — every last one. So let's get going." He waved for Elwood to follow and turned the boat for the beach again, opening the throttle.

Elwood made no effort to move from his position. He just turned his head and stared after the boat until Bill eventually turned around and motored back. The two silently unloaded the groceries while the airplane and the rusted boat bumped and banged together in the swell.

The last box of groceries went into the battered boat and Elwood climbed into his seat, preparing to leave.

"Oh," he said, pulling an envelope from his pocket and handing it down. "Blackie gave me this; said be sure you got it."

Bill took the grease-stained envelope and ripped it open, read the terse note it contained:

> Bill, I'll take my favor now. One good — and I mean good — red cedar log. Length 40 feet minimum. Girth 16 feet. Delivered. Keep quiet about this, and don't tell me you can't find one neither.
> *Blackie*

Meanwhile, in town, pounding and sawing sounds were emerging from Blackie's garage. The noise raised no eyebrows on Main Street. Blackie always had projects going in the old building at all hours of the day and night — or his friends did.

This time the noise heralded an expansion. Blackie was building a partition out of rough lumber and canvas, dividing the shop. He left space in front for the occasional car repair job. In the partition he put an old wooden door and on it he hung a sign that said, "Private — No Entry."

Later, when anyone asked him what was behind the door, Blackie said he was going to build a boat in there to go back to fishing, but that for the meantime it was just a junkhole.

Blackie expanded the working space of the new shop by building a tent on wooden frames over the old loading dock at the rear. The dock was connected to the shop with double doors, which Blackie and Mickey dismantled. From the harbor side Blackie's place looked like a gypsy camp, but nobody gave it a second thought. After all, it *was* Blackie's.

On a rainy night ten days after he received the note, Bill stomped up the stairs to Blackie's apartment and pounded on the door. Blackie opened up and peered outside.

"Got your log," Bill said. "Where do you want her?"

Two hours later, on the high tide, Blackie and Bill jerked the big log from the bay up into the building, using Blackie's old tow truck.

Next day, Mickey hurried down after school. He and Blackie looked at the tree on the floor. It took up the length of the room and stuck out into the tent. It was always chilly in the building except sometimes in midsummer, but the massive log, fresh from the woods and from a twenty-mile trip behind Bill's iron boat, made it seem forebodingly damp and cold.

Blackie ducked into the office and returned with a cylinder of drafting paper. He unrolled the paper onto the workbench, weighted it down, and showed Mickey a working sketch of the canoe. It looked for all the world like the one Mickey had seen in his dream, right down to the carved decorations and the graceful bird-neck of a reaching bow. It startled him.

"Me and the wife drew it up last night," Blackie said. "The wife, she knows a thing or two about canoes."

Mickey took the paper reverently and tacked it to the wall

where the filtered light from the dirty windows struck it and made it look ancient and weathered. Then he took a hatchet from the workbench and walked to the log. He struck a chip from it.

"First lick," he said to Blackie.

"First one," replied Blackie. "But you gonna need more than that-there hatchet, chile."

Blackie reached under the workbench, pulled out a huge chain saw, started it and, humming to the high wail of the saw, began on the log.

7

is real name was Scott-Blair. As a young newspaper reporter in England he had decided to kick over the traces and take up a gypsy life. His aim was to work at his profession in as many countries as he could in his lifetime. He decided that when a place began to look especially charming or a woman entered the picture and things got serious — that would be the signal to pack up and move on to the next job. And so it had been.

He had worked in New Zealand on several papers, then he had signed on as crew on a yacht, crossed the Tasman Sea and taken up the work in Australia. He tried Fiji, moved on to Papeete and finally found himself in Mexico City, where he wrote for an English-language newspaper and learned the Spanish language and the art of lounging in sidewalk cafes, reading newspapers and sipping dry red wines, while the insane traffic poured down the boulevard nearby. When Mexico

City began to get complicated and attractive beyond the normal, he traveled north, spending a year in Sonora before he decided the Mexican sun had baked him enough and Alaska was just the place for him to be.

Now *The Citizen* and the little island town it served were decidedly first in Editor's heart and he had conceded this might be the longest stay in the lot. Sometimes when the sun came and turned Southeastern Alaska into a glittering wonderland of water and trees and mountains, Scott-Blair suspected this stay might be forever.

Editor brought to town a classical education along with his international journalistic experience. That he might be grossly overqualified to run the little *Citizen* never entered the thoughts of his neighbors and readers; they just accepted this thoughtful, soft-spoken and quite obviously gifted and experienced newspaperman as they accepted any other individual who cared to share the tip of Wrangell Island with them summer and winter — as a neighbor.

So Editor fitted in nicely and he was a happy and challenged man. He worked terribly long hours at *The Citizen*, but broke them up with little excursions through town when he chatted with his readers and friends, giving special attention to children and the old. He addressed all dogs as "Old Chum." Some of the dogs sensed something special in Editor and trailed along joyously with him on his treks. He strode along with graceful, long strides, and he would breathe deeply and swing his arms round and round, making the children laugh, in an exercise regimen he told them "gets blood to my brain," making them laugh more and louder. Editor wore either one of two expensive tweed jackets he owned and which had seen much wear through the years. He kept a green eyeshade perched on his head and a long-stemmed curved pipe clamped between his teeth. He was a bachelor, but sometimes women came into his life. He also took an occasional nip while "collecting news" at the Wrangell Inn across Main Street from *The Citizen* office.

Editor was such an unassuming and seemingly defenseless and guileless man that Wrangell, sometimes slow in warming to newcomers, made him one of its own almost overnight. He was soon on a first-name basis with nearly everyone in town, ranging all the way from the nabobs who thought they were at the top of the heap to assorted others who labored in the woods and on the water and inside the tin-sided, smoking, clanking mill.

There is an old saw that says folks won't bother to give a nickname to a man unless they like him — or despise him. In Editor's case it was the former by a flat-out landslide. In fact, he came by the simple nickname "Editor" his very first night in town. It probably was some sort of record, but no one kept track of such a statistic in Wrangell.

It was raining when Scott-Blair coaxed his battered Chevy three-quarter-ton truck off the ferry and up the ramp to the Wrangell shore. The rig had seen a hundred thousand miles and more of the United States, Mexico, South America and Canada and it was tired, but still game. The faded coach mounted in the truck bed sat high behind the cab. The coach was jammed with the paraphernalia of Scott-Blair's gypsy life — books, cameras, fishing gear, cartons of canned goods, half a jug of Vino Tinto from Mexico, a heavy filing cabinet lashed in a corner and stuffed with fiction and journals Scott-Blair intended to do something with someday. A tall, forty-year-old black Underwood typewriter rode on the floor between the coach's two little facing sofas.

When Scott-Blair's rig finally lurched to a stop outside the terminal building and he ran inside to ask his way to the newspaper, the town knew the latest editor was on the island. They were not particularly impressed or hopeful. After all, this newcomer was just the most recent of a string of incompetent pretenders. None lasted more than a few issues of the paper and their efforts were a sad commentary on their abilities — the poor *Citizen*, once one of Alaska's finest, was fallen on hard times indeed.

Scott-Blair drove slowly through the downpour and found the newspaper office. It was locked, but he slipped the door with a knife blade, got the dirty lightbulb glowing, and for the first time laid eyes on his new love.

He wasn't disappointed. He saw through it all instantly. "Hello there," he said aloud. "Oh my, just what I expected."

The old, high-ceilinged room smelled mustily of a half-century of ink and paper. The memories of the creative work that had gone on there somehow lingered. It was quiet and the bad light cast shadows over the covered, sorry typesetting gear and the few dusty desks and shelves. A rack of old *Citizen*s going back more than eighty years was set against one wall, dust and cobwebs making the legends on the bindings impossible to read. Outside, the night had turned black and a dismal rain drummed on the street and on the tin marquee of *The Citizen* building, and dripped from rusty gutters, splaying patterns on the front windows. Scott-Blair didn't care. He took a deep, satisfied breath, lit his old curved pipe and sailed around, ripping off machine covers, trying out the office typewriter and finally puttering in the makeshift darkroom, where he found a box of old-fashioned four-by-five negatives. These occupied him for a full hour. He sat on a stool and looked at the transparent sheets of history against the room's one bare lightbulb, shaking his head in delight and wonder and saying, "My, my. My word. Wonderful!" Then he turned to the back issues and his spirits really soared. In years past *The Citizen* had been edited by a string of really first-rate journalists whose sense of history was as fine-tuned as Scott-Blair's. Reading these words, many written before Scott-Blair was born, he realized that *The Citizen*, though fallen in grace and tatty at present, was once a great little newspaper.

"Yes," thought the journalist, "I stand by that. It was a great paper. And it shall be again — as fine as I can make it." And with that pronouncement, he turned off the light, pulled the door shut behind him and crossed the rain-slicked street to the Wrangell Inn.

Scott-Blair chatted amiably with his companions. The bar patrons at first answered the stranger's comments in grunts or not at all, but finally he won them over with his wide-eyed openness. They warmed up, accepted him as a drinking companion — a "mate," as Scott-Blair explained to them how it would be in an Australian pub. But it was understood among the inn crowd — well understood — that this *was* Saturday night and when jostling started about midnight, as it must start, the newcomer would have to take what came. For anyone with the temerity to stick around Wrangell Inn until that hour on Saturday shouldn't, after all, expect less. No one thought to tell the Englishman what would happen. It was the Wrangell way.

The bar was located at the west end of a half-block-long frame building, which also housed hotel rooms and a restaurant. Its big windows overlooked Sumner Strait, which at night showed up as a black void and in the daylight as a shining waterway leading west to the sea and east to the mouth of the mighty Stikine River. Revelers bellied up to a high, L-shaped bar or lounged at one of a dozen round-topped tables scattered around the room.

Scott-Blair was at the bar and feeling two-drink comfortable at the appointed hour. Suddenly, at precisely midnight by the bar clock, a craggy-faced Irish-Tlingit fisherman named O'Ryan downed his fifth mixed drink in one gulp, pushed his glass back with a satisfied sigh, and insulted the young, squarely built millworker perched on the barstool next to him. The millworker, who came by his pugnaciousness honestly, having played four hard years of university football, simply reached out one massive arm and swept O'Ryan over backward, barstool and all.

With that, bedlam broke out and in a twinkling the room took on the appearance of a Keystone Kops movie. Patrons were swinging, yelling, laughing and falling. Music blared from the jukebox. A tree-faller named Bob-the-Bear grasped Scott-Blair from behind by the collar, but in the melee somehow ended up sprinting awkwardly backward across the room until he fetched up with a terrific jolt against a wall. Bob, who had never been off his feet in a brawl, looked sheepishly around him, shook his head, scrambled up and charged back to the bar and Scott-Blair. Somehow the big logger found himself back at the wall again, sitting on the same piece of floor he had so recently occupied.

Soon loggers, millworkers and fishermen all seemed to be approaching and leaving the newspaperman's general locale, and, as if by some form of legerdemain, sailing through the air or sliding out of control across the floor, to fetch up with crashes or thuds against furniture or walls. In the general confusion, the smiling Englishman never seemed to be really involved, only clumsily defensive. It looked as if he were trying hard to keep from getting hit or grasped, and that was all. He definitely looked out of place in a barroom brawl at midnight in Alaska, with his tweed jacket, his curved pipe still smouldering between his teeth, and a thin smile on his mouth.

When the bartender eventually blinked the house lights three times and then hurtled into the center of the room, a bottle in each hand and a dire look in his eyes, and called time, Scott-Blair was the only man still standing at the bar. The revelers returned to the business of drinking, and the bartender eyed Scott-Blair curiously, perhaps a little knowingly.

"Sorry," the barman said, "it gets this way sometimes. The gladiators get going at midnight Saturdays — it's their day. A tradition, you might say. I call them gladiators. You hurt?"

"Really," said Scott-Blair in his broadest accent. "Really quite extraordinary. I was almost too frightened to move. Dear me. Nobody bothered me. Quite all right. My, my." He smiled at the bartender from behind his now-dead pipe and busied himself looking for tobacco and matches in the pockets of his jacket.

The barman arched his eyebrows, swiped the bartop with a wet towel, and eyed the newspaperman closely. "Yeah," he said. "Yeah." He leaned across the bar, his face close to Scott-Blair's. "Say, how about I just call you Editor from now on — that be okay?"

Scott-Blair gave the barman a dazzling smile. "Indeed so!" he said. "I would consider it an honor, a compliment."

And so from then on that was how it was — Scott-Blair became "Editor" and the name fit, for he was one, and a good one, and he stayed in Wrangell and plied his trade in the old office. And *The Citizen*, with Editor at the helm, prospered and began to regain its quality.

8

om Lincoln learned carving as a boy. His teacher was his ancient uncle, who had learned the craft from his own uncle, who had actually seen the Russians land.

Tom's uncle worked in a clapboard, ramshackle shack by the harbor before his death. The shack was bright and warm inside, heated by a crackling barrel stove that burned wood chips. Tourists came off the ferries and tour ships in the summers to make pilgrimages to the shack of the old Tlingit carver of Wrangell. They bought his decorated canoe paddles and wood images of fish, frogs and ravens and carried these treasures proudly back aboard their ships to take home.

Once, Tom's uncle found a suitable cedar log adrift in the bay, towed it ashore, winched it into his shack and carved a little canoe. The old man presented the canoe to his nephew with much ceremony, on the condition that Tom would not drown himself, and bade him to go voyaging — but not too far from shore. Tom paddled the canoe around the bay and learned to carve and thought about one day succeeding his uncle as the town's carver. But it was not to be.

Tom Lincoln gravitated instead to logging, felling trees in the summer and spending his winters in idle ease in his late uncle's house by the shop. The shop itself was mostly silent now, its stove cold. The tools were still racked there neatly. Sometimes Tom would go and sit in the shack and think about when he was a boy in that place.

■ ■ ■

It was raining hard when Tom Lincoln, his massive bulk wrapped with an old piece of tarp, raced up the stairs to Blackie's apartment and banged on the door. When Tom entered the smoky interior, Blackie thrust a mug of coffee in the logger's hand, and when he had warmed up a bit, they adjourned to the shop below.

When he saw the log there, Tom Lincoln whistled. "I'll be, Blackie. By golly . . ."

Then the carver moved slowly to the log and, one hand trailing along the cool wood, walked its length slowly, whispering to himself, "By golly, I'll be . . ."

He walked around the log two times, never lifting his hand from it, inspected the ends carefully, and finally stopped near Blackie, who stood, arms folded, watching. Tom Lincoln said, "Okay, I'll help you — you have to know exactly how to do this, Blackie."

"Didn't ask for no help — yet," growled Blackie.

"You'd hafta," said Tom Lincoln. "This ain't just a

darned chain-saw job, Blackie. This is . . . well, it's special. It's gotta be done just right or not at all."

"I got it roughed out, see," said Blackie. "Tom, I'm afeared to cut another lick offen her," he admitted.

"Yeah," said Tom Lincoln, then added absently, now staring at the canoe plan tacked to the wall. "Boiling water. We gotta scoop her out, then we've gotta fill her up with boiling water and coax her shape in real careful and slow. Back when my uncle was a boy the way they did it was, they filled the log with seawater and then they heated up rocks in a big fire and threw the rocks in the log. When they got her good and soft they warped her into the shape they wanted, using wooden braces. It's not all that simple but we can do it."

Blackie started to reply, then checked himself, for the carver had walked slowly away and was back at the canoe, down on his knees, an adz in his hands. He was making careful cuts, watching the cedar curl away before his blade.

■ ■ ■

Waldo Bernet was taking his history class on another trip into the past. Now, though, the students were following willingly.

"No one knows," said Bernet, waving his long arms passionately before him, "for how many centuries the Tlingits ruled this land before the Russian Chirikov showed up that day in 1741 on a voyage of exploration."

The teacher gazed across the roofs of the town to a wind-tossed strait and beyond to the dark, timbered islands, where waves dashed white against their beaches. The islands marched thus, he knew, some eighty-eight watery miles to the open ocean from which the Russians had suddenly appeared a mere two hundred and some-odd years previously. Their arrival marked the beginning of a conquest that not only cost the Tlingit his rule over the archipelago, but cost him also his culture and ultimately his past, and therefore much of his identity.

Bernet drew from his rich imagination and keen scholarship the story of that first ship, sent by Peter the Great, as she timidly approached a wholly unknown, terrifying, tantalizing shore. Bernet related in an excited whisper the first brief and pathetic contact.

"The crew wanted to go ashore for water," he said, "but it was foreboding. Captain Chirikov sent a boat in with ten armed men. They disappeared. He waited two days — what agony that must have been! He sent a smaller boat after the first. Four men manned it. They were lost — gone. No clues. The ship sailed away without attempting another landing. Who knew what terrors those forests held? What happened to those sailors was never learned."

"The Tlingits got 'em," said a boy, and then the class was a babble of released emotion. Dr. Bernet gazed at them, delighted.

Mickey raised his hand. "Canoes, Dr. Bernet. What about canoes?"

"Ah, yes," said the teacher. "Important in the Tlingit culture, as you can imagine — as you know. They were the only transportation they had. The only method. Who of you has tried to walk along the beaches or through the woods here? Cannot be done with any dispatch or comfort. Water transport was the only way of getting from place to place. Now we have airplanes, but we don't have roads that go far, do we?"

Bernet went to his desk and searched for a minute, then carried a picture to the bulletin board and pinned it up. It was of a Tlingit war canoe. Mickey's heart jumped at the sight of it. The canoe, with two companion canoes, was under a small square sail and was running before a blustery wind between high mountains. It was a wild scene, and beautiful.

"Canoes," Bernet said, pointing at the picture. "Those beautiful vessels hewn from logs into graceful forms. They were the Tlingits' most treasured possessions. Oh, most valuable. They were almost alive, weren't they? The canoes, as they skimmed those waters out there — can't you imagine them?"

Bernet gestured at Sumner Strait. The surface danced and shimmered under rays of a sun beginning to penetrate low-hanging clouds. The light came warmly into the old classroom for an instant and struck Dr. Bernet, who stood with eyes moist and glowing before his beloved students. He looked strikingly, to Mickey, like pictures he had seen of old John Muir, the naturalist who himself so loved Wrangell and Alaska.

■■■

Mickey was having more and more trouble with Tim Sipe. The bigger boy had not forgotten the incident on Main Street. He accosted Mickey at every opportunity — in the hallways at school, in town when they chanced to meet. That a combat would be the ultimate result of the book incident, Mickey had no doubt. He also had little doubt about the outcome of a battle with Tim Sipe. Meanwhile, he avoided the boy as far as possible and was beginning to live in that terrible state of fear familiar to boys through the ages with exactly the same problem.

Having an enemy ready to strike at any time did not diminish Mickey's fervor for the canoe project, however. He showed up each day after school on schedule and worked on the log as directed now by Tom Lincoln. The log was looking less and less like a log and more and more like a canoe.

The craft and Mickey's plans to sail it into the midst of the town's famous Fourth of July celebration — for that was his intent from the first — were a well-kept secret. Well-kept secret, so far. But Editor was getting curious. One day the newspaperman hailed Blackie on the street, asking bluntly what was going on in the back of Blackie's shop.

"Ah," the garageman replied, his eyes smoky, "mebbe jus' a little old project."

Editor let it drop but a week later he collared Blackie again. "You know, I've done a bit of research on that building of yours. It was a saloon and billiard parlor in the Gold Rush."

Blackie raised an eyebrow. "Do tell," he said. "I thought it smelled like booze."

"I want to do a story on the building," Editor persisted. "I'll be down to get some pictures."

"Not this week," Blackie replied, flashing Editor a hard smile. "Busy."

So it went until one day Editor slammed through the front door of the garage, a camera in his hand, and announced he was ready to get to work.

Blackie was blunt. "Busy," he said, and turned away.

Editor, looking hurt, persisted. He said he had no intention of leaving until Blackie came clean.

Finally the garageman shrugged and told Editor, "We're doin' something secret. We're not telling you nothin' so stop pushin'."

"I shan't write about it, then," said Editor. "I promise I won't write a word unless you say so and until you say so. Show me." Editor looked hopefully at Blackie.

"Nope."

"Oh, dear, this is awkward," said Editor. He turned slowly and left the garage, trudging back to his office through the rain. But he was back the next afternoon, and the next after that, and on each afternoon for a week. Work on the canoe came almost to a standstill. Finally the decision was made.

"We can trust him," said Blackie to Mickey and Tom. "I knew them limeys when I was in the war. They got whatcha-callit — inter-grady."

"Integrity," corrected Mickey.

"That's it," said Blackie. "He won't tell nobody."

When Editor came in that afternoon, Mickey said simply, "It's a canoe. A real big one."

"My word," said Editor. "Let's have a look." He pushed his way past the two and disappeared through the greasy door to the back.

Editor walked the length of the log, trailing his hand over the wood just as Tom Lincoln had done. He gazed at the drawing tacked to the wall and he looked carefully at the picture Mickey showed him in the book.

"You know," Editor said, "this could be a big story." He held up a hand. "Mind you, I wouldn't say or write a thing until I got the word."

Mickey told Editor that he had learned about canoes and how this one would astonish Wrangell and make the Native community proud when it skimmed out across the bay on the Fourth.

Editor listened intently, looked at the log for a long time, then walked to the workbench and picked up an adz.

"I'm not a Native, Mickey," Editor said, "but I wonder

if it would be proper to let me have the honor of assisting in this project in a most practical way?"

"He means he wants to take a whack at it with that-there blade," Blackie said.

"Indeed yes," said Editor. "I should remember it all my life — that I helped if only a little, to fashion this canoe. May I, Mickey?"

So that was how Editor became part of the scheme. He was a frequent visitor to the shop, watching Blackie, Mickey and Tom Lincoln labor on the canoe.

One day while the four sat around the office stove, Blackie said to Editor: "I heered through the grapevine that you could sling fellas around in fights. There's this story about you up to the inn. Any truth to that-there?"

"Not a word," said Editor, smiling. "Do I appear to be the combative type, Blackie?"

"Mmmmmm," said Blackie. "I've met fellers who didn't look too tough. They was, though."

"If it was true," Mickey chimed in. "If it was true that you could sling fellas around like they say. Maybe with karate or something. Could you teach me a couple of things? I have a problem with a guy."

"Indeed no," said Editor. "If I could do that, what you say, what earthly purpose would it serve to teach it to a schoolboy so he could perhaps injure another schoolboy?"

"Oh, I don't want to hurt this guy much," said Mickey. "Just sling him off the dock or something."

Editor looked startled.

"Don't worry," said Mickey. "He can swim."

"What sort of problem?" Editor asked. "And what sort of bloke might this be who deserves such a chilling undoing?"

Mickey told his story. As it unfolded, a stern look came into Editor's face. Shortly he, Mickey, Blackie and Tom Lincoln adjourned to the shop. Blackie and Tom went immediately to work, Mickey and Editor found a clear, private corner, from which scufflings and resounding thumps and thuds could be heard now and then over the whine of the saw and the whack of the adz and hatchet.

Blackie nodded as he labored, smiled, and hummed tunelessly.

ditor, while accepted by Wrangell as a solid and useful citizen, an Alaskan, nevertheless remained a mystery. Where he had been and what he had been he never discussed. That he could speak Spanish became general town knowledge when a Mexican-American visited Wrangell and he and Editor fell into the tongue most comfortable for the guest. Oblivious to the stares and amused grins of passersby, the pair carried on an animated, arm-waving conversation one sunny afternoon outside *The Citizen* and then continued it at the Wrangell Inn far into the night.

"Editor's in the saloon carrying on in some foreign lingo with a guy," a logger reported to another.

"He's something, that Editor," said the second man. "Never know what that limey's going to do next."

That was true. The full view of Editor's

personality would never come out if he stayed in Wrangell fifty years. He was not by nature a secretive man, just a private one. The town knew he was capable as a journalist through the quality of the newspaper. Children and animals knew by instinct Editor was kind, and Blackie, who was alert to such things, guessed accurately at the source of Editor's soldierly bearing.

Mickey just knew deep in his soul that he needed and wanted the man's respect and friendship and sought both, actively and without shame.

And so it happened that one day Editor spied Mickey passing outside the newspaper's front window and, acting on impulse, called the boy back and steered him in. He sat Mickey at the scarred desk where he wrote his news and editorials and thought up advertising campaigns for local stores (a side of newspaper ownership he abhorred). Editor took a seat opposite the boy and folded his long-fingered hands in front of him.

"I like you," he began, "but I'm worried, lad. It seems you've gotten off on the wrong path."

Mickey stared at Editor. "About the canoe?" he ventured.

"No, the canoe's fine. About you."

"Me."

Mickey grew suddenly uncomfortable. The newspaperman was boring through him with steady blue eyes. Though he had no basis to feel it, the boy imagined himself a recalcitrant soldier being dressed down by his officer.

Mickey thought to escape. "Gotta go," he began, starting to rise.

Editor held out an arm in a gesture that dropped the boy back into his chair. Mickey noticed for the first time the knotted arm muscles and a hard, no-nonsense glint in Editor's eyes.

"Lad, I've heard the tales. Terrible. You are troublesome.

Smoking in school, alcohol arrests, foul language and more and more. Since grade school you've been in trouble. What IS the story?"

Mickey shrugged and stared silently at the desk top.

Editor continued: "So you happen to be an Indian and . . ."

"Native!" Mickey shouted, rising to his full height and knocking his chair over with a crash. "Tlingit. We used to kill Englishmen like you and cut 'em up." The boy leaned forward over the desk, genuinely angered at the man.

Editor leaned back in his chair easily and said, "Well, well, well. I think I'm beginning to see."

"See what?" Mickey countered. "See nothin'. You see nothin'."

"Poor lad. All these years of hostility. Put off because you are Native when you should be proud of it. Is that it? We must talk. Sit down."

Mickey sat, his anger melting into confusion.

"How would you like to be at the top of your class?" Editor asked.

"Funny," mumbled the boy.

"You're not a dull lad, Mickey," said Editor. "Indeed, I believe you to be a bright one. You act like a dunce and a hoodlum. What a devil of a lot of trouble that must be for you."

"Ahhh," said Mickey.

"Indeed, all this must have something to do with your race, your home life or both — I don't care why. I just regret seeing a mind wasted. In fact, in this case, I forbid it."

Mickey was suddenly angry again. "You don't own me. You can't make me study — or do anything." He stared angrily into Editor's eyes, but it was useless. Editor's return gaze was that of a better, stronger man and a friend all in one. Mickey looked away, unable to hold the contact. When he looked back his eyes were swimming.

"There now," said Editor quietly. "There now." Then he smiled. "Right. Now, here's how we must go about this. . . ."

■ ■ ■

The light glowed yellow behind the windows of Tom Lincoln's shop as Mickey trudged along muddy Harbor Street. It was early evening and a cold rain misted down.

Inside it was warm. The barrel stove was glowing again and Tom Lincoln looked content and startlingly like his old uncle as he shaved wood and squinted and shaved some more at the paddle he was fashioning.

"That's going to be beautiful," Mickey said. The paddle of glowing yellow cedar was a full five feet long and Tom Lincoln had roughed out an elaborate decorative design on it.

"I have to make a lot of these to move that canoe," he laughed. "But, you know, Mickey, I'm enjoying this. My uncle would have smiled at all of this." He looked approvingly around the interior of the old shack, at the neat rows of tools on the wall, at the cluttered workbench and at the supply of wood he had moved in for the work he was to do over the coming months.

The plan was to have twenty paddlers in the canoe and each a Native. Each would want a paddle as grand as any of his neighbors', and Tom Lincoln chuckled at this. "We're liable to have a war on our hands when we pick the paddlers," he said. "But then the rest who want to can ride, I expect. We'll make them honorary chiefs."

Mickey took a seat on a sawhorse and kicked idly at the

wood chips on the plank floor. He was feeling curiously at home in this old place.

"Tell me about your uncle," he said suddenly to Tom Lincoln.

Tom looked up from his work and said, "He was the last of the old carvers in Wrangell. He knew all the old ways and he knew where all the old totems were and what they meant. He could carve a totem, and he did." Tom Lincoln's voice trailed off and he stared into the distance through the wall of his uncle's shack, back across the rainy, windy years. "He was a Tlingit and proud of it," he almost whispered to Mickey. "Very proud. . . ."

■ ■ ■

Tom Lincoln was a boy and he was listening to his uncle and aunt chatter away in the guttural Tlingit tongue as his aunt cooked a fragrant meal on her wood stove and his uncle smoked. Occasionally the two would revert to English, then swing effortlessly back to Tlingit. Tom was sleepily catching the exchange.

" 'Dogs and Indians Not Allowed'," his uncle was saying with disgust. "That is what the sign said, and I can still see it. It was in the window of a restaurant, understand. I was a little shaver but I could read by then." His uncle had shaken his head slowly, sadly, remembering, still after all those years unable to understand the cruelty of the sign and what it stood for.

"No wonder the language is dying out. How can we expect it to be different?" he demanded of Tom's aunt, who grunted a reply and shook her head and continued cooking. "No mystery that our old ways are being forgotten and, worse, ridiculed and scorned by our young. My own father and mother said to us children that perhaps we should learn only English, forget about Tlingit. They said that to speak Tlingit brought trouble with whites. And they themselves spoke both Tlingit and Haida and had been raised in the old ways. They knew and revered the traditions, yet they were ready to throw them away. Our culture! Our own culture, you understand. That is why it is dying — is all but dead." His uncle had lapsed into silence then, behind his pipe, an old Tlingit carver with misting eyes and fading memories.

Tom Lincoln resumed his work at the cedar paddle, gazing across his uncle's shop at the boy.

"Were Tlingits pretty tough?" Mickey asked.

Tom looked at the boy who lounged there, noting the squared-off shoulders still hardening in growth, the piercing black eyes under a strong forehead and severe brows.

"Yes," said the carver. "They were brave and strong and fierce and full of pride. They lived by a code in force for centuries before ever the white man came here. The pride caused a lot of trouble for a long time, Mickey. The Native learned that he must live by white man's rules finally, or die — like Scutdoo."

Mickey leaned forward, the glow of the fire flickering yellow over his dark face. "Scutdoo," he said. "Tell me about Scutdoo, Tom."

10

om put his tools carefully on the workbench and took a seat opposite the boy.

"I'll tell you the story of the hanging of Scutdoo exactly as my uncle was told it," he said. "I heard it many times. I remember it almost to the very words used by the Tlingit who first told it — he who was there and who saw it — before it came down word-of-mouth to my uncle. It happened when the Americans came to rule Alaska. It happened when they finally came to Wrangell:

"In the fall of 1869, white soldiers arrived in Wrangell. They hired our people to cut logs to build a fort where the Federal Building now stands. All the time our people work, work, work and by Christmas they have built two log houses and one, another big one where the captain lives, of lumber. Around all this they built a big yard — a stockade — of logs with a big double gate.

"There are two towns then in Wrangell. One the white man's town, the fort, and the other the Indians' town.

"The white soldiers' houses and fort are done.

"On Christmas Eve, the captain of the fort sends word to all the chiefs of the Indian villages: 'What is that for, Christmas Eve?' Our interpreter does not know. The Indians do not know. They have never heard of Christmas. They don't know, then, about Christ being born. They just know the white chief of the soldiers say it is a time to be happy.

"Nighttime comes. It is cold. The wind blows. Raining. Snowing. The Indians go up the beach to the fort. Inside the captain's house everything is warm. Lights. Music. The soldiers are playing a violin and accordion.

"When you come in the door of the captain's house there is a big stair going up to a wide hall. At the bottom of the stair are two doors opening to rooms off the entry hall. In one of these rooms is the captain's wife. She does not come to the party upstairs. She stays in the room.

"The Indians go upstairs.

"Among the Indians are two brothers named Isteen and Chuwan. They are nephews of Towaatt, one of the chiefs of the Indian village. They have their wives. Isteen's wife is Aglan. She is from the south. At Victoria she has seen white people. She knows white men's dances and has on a dress like white ladies wear. It is wide with hoops and when the other Indians see her their eyes pop for they have never seen such a dress. Aglan, too, she knows how to do the white man's quadrille, which she learned at the fort in Victoria.

"Kchok-een, she is the other brother's wife, Chuwan's wife. She is a pretty Indian girl with rosy cheeks, but she wears only Indian clothes, moccasins and has a blanket around her. She does not know how to dance like this Aglan.

"The Indians sit on benches around the wall of the big hall. The soldiers pass plates of sandwiches and much wine. Wine? The Indians do not know what is wine. Pretty soon everybody's head is going 'round. Indians' and soldiers'.

"Pretty soon the captain comes and says to Aglan. 'We dance?' Aglan then dances with the white captain and all the Indians sit surprised to see Aglan dancing so nice with the white chief. Then, another soldier asks Kchok-een to dance. Kchok-een does not know how to dance like Aglan but she gets up and tries. Soon, everyone around is laughing at Kchok-een trying to dance like Aglan. All the white chiefs are laughing, laughing.

"Kchok-een's husband sees his wife, and everybody laughing at her, and he gets very mad. He is much ashamed that everybody should laugh at his wife. He steps out onto the dance floor and pulls her away from the white soldier and throws her down the stairs. Kchok-een falls over and over to the bottom of the stairs. She screams. Then, down below, the captain's wife, who is in this room at the bottom of the stairs, hears Kchok-een scream. She rushes out into the hall and quick picks up Kchok-een and takes her into the room. But before she can close the door, Chuwan, who is a big, strong fellow, comes down the stairs. He wants his wife. He wants to send her home so she cannot be laughed at anymore. He pulls at the door. It comes open a little way and the captain's wife puts her hand against Chuwan's face to shove him back and Chuwan bites off her finger.

"Now the captain's wife screams and all the soldiers from above rush down the stairs. There is the captain's wife holding her hand and the blood pouring down her arm. The captain steps forward. He is very mad. He tells the soldiers to shoot Chuwan down. Isteen tries to save his brother and the soldiers shoot both the brothers down. Chuwan falls, shot through the heart, and the other brother, shot through the arm, dies later.

"Now, Indians are scared. They fly out the front door and out into the dark, cold rain and snow outside. They run quick for their homes across town in the Native village.

"Later that night soldiers come to Towaatt's house. Towaatt, then, has a house near where the Wrangell sawmill is now. The soldiers say to Towaatt, 'Towaatt, you want to fight?' But Towaatt sits very still. He says nothing. The soldiers go home. Tramp, tramp, they march down the beach back to the fort.

"Not far from Towaatt lives the brothers' father, Scutdoo. He is asleep while his sons have been killed. But his wife, when she hears of it, wakes him. She shakes his shoulder and says, 'Scutdoo, the white soldiers have killed our sons. Wake up, your sons are dead. What are you going to do?'

"Scutdoo gets up. He dresses. He puts on his red war jacket. I remember it well. I have seen it many times. It is all red and has pockets around the bottom for shells for his Hudson's Bay gun. Scutdoo gets his Hudson's Bay gun and starts for the fort. He walks along the beach and it is still cold and windy, half raining, half snowing. He walks, walks.

"Along the beach lives Leon Smith. He has a trading post. He is the only white man in Wrangell who lives outside the fort. He has a long log cabin with a porch across the front.

"Scutdoo walks, walks. Pretty soon he comes to Smith's trading post. He sees Smith walking across his porch. Well, here is a white man. Indians' law says that when one of their men is killed by another tribe, other tribe must pay with the life of one of their men. White men have killed Scutdoo's sons. Here is a white man. So, Scutdoo raises his Hudson's Bay gun and shoots. Smith falls dead.

"As soon as he has killed Smith, Scutdoo becomes afraid. Quick he runs through the storm into the woods behind Wrangell to hide.

"The next day there is big trouble. The captain of the fort comes down to the Indian village. He says, 'Where is the man that killed Smith? I want that man!' But the Indians do not know where Scutdoo has gone. He is somewhere in the woods up back of Wrangell. The captain says, 'If you don't get that man who has killed Smith and bring him to me, I will turn my cannons on the town. I will shoot up every house in your village.'

"Everybody is scared. At that time there are many Indian houses in the villages. Kakes, Tsimpsians, many Indians from all around have moved to Wrangell to work for the white soldiers cutting wood for the fort. They are scared. Everybody is scared.

"The soldiers go back to the fort. Pretty soon — boom! We all hear the cannons of the fort. Boom! A cannonball has gone straight through Scutdoo's house and knocked it down.

"Now, Chief Shakes, who is the head chief, gets mad. He rushes to Towaatt's house. He says, 'Towaatt, we are going to the fort. We will talk to the white chief. The soldiers have killed two of our men. We have killed one of theirs. We will take one soldier and kill him and then everything will be even.' Shakes was plenty mad.

"Shakes is all dressed up like the soldiers. He has a uniform with gold bunches on its shoulders and he has a long sword at his side. He has another soldier suit, so he makes Towaatt put it on and they go to the fort. They march along the beach up to the fort. The gates are closed, but they tell the sentry they want to see his chief. The captain says, 'Let them come in.'

"In the captain's office the captain says for them to sit down but Shakes says, 'No.' The captain then says, 'What do you want, Shakes?' Shakes says, 'One man. Your man who killed my friend, Chuwan, and then I will give you Scutdoo who killed Smith.'

"The captain says nothing. He sits and thinks. After a while he says, 'Shakes, wait for a while. Our law says we must have the man who killed Smith, but you go home. I will think it over.'

"Shakes and Towaatt go home then. The next day comes and the captain has said nothing. Then Shakes gets mad again. He is very mad. He goes to Towaatt's house. This time he does not go in. He just kicks the door open and says, 'Towaatt, come! We will go take a soldier and kill him. Are you going to do nothing?'

"But Towaatt, who is a very smart and peaceful man, says to Shakes, 'Brother, our chief, let them go. They are a big dog. We are only a little dog. If we take a soldier and kill him, they will kill all the Wrangell people. Let them go, my brother.'

"Shakes gets more mad. He slams the door. 'You coward,' he says. Shakes wants to fight the soldiers.

"That day Scutdoo comes down out of the woods. For two nights he has been hiding. Nothing to eat. Nothing to keep him warm. He has heard the guns of the fort firing on the Indian village. He is going to give himself up. He goes around to different houses of the villages. He says to his friends, 'Let us smoke, I am going to die. I am going to give myself up to the soldiers.' He goes to his brother-in-law Shustak's house and says, 'Let us eat our last meal together. I want to eat here before I die.' Scutdoo eats a little smoked salmon, then he smokes, then he gives his gun to his brother-in-law and takes a canoe and sets out across the bay for the fort. 'I go to give myself up,' he says. 'If I do not give myself up, you will all die.'

"In the fort yard the soldiers have built a gallows. As soon as they have Scutdoo, the captain sends word to the Indian villages. He invites all the people to come and see how they hang a man.

"Scutdoo is a composer. He sends word for his mother to bring his dancing hat so he can sing and dance once more before he dies. His mother brings the hat. She is crying. She has put a knife in his dancing hat hoping that her son can kill the men who want to kill him. But when the soldiers give Scutdoo his dancing hat the knife is gone. Scutdoo puts on his dancing hat and he dances and sings a song he has composed.

"As soon as he has finished, he gives his mother his dancing hat. He turns and walks stiff and straight up the steps to the platform where the soldiers are waiting. The soldiers start to put a cloth over Scutdoo's face. They have the rope ready. But Scutdoo will not have a cloth over his head. He tears the cloth away. The soldiers put the rope around his neck. Everything is quiet except for Scutdoo's old mother. She is crying and Indians stand around in the rain looking very sad. Scutdoo is their brother.

"The soldiers wait a minute. But Scutdoo does not wait. He does not wait for them to, how do you say it — spring the trap? No, Scutdoo will not wait. He jumps off the high platform. And so he dies."*

His long story ended, Tom Lincoln sighed, rose, slowly gathered up his tools and returned to work. Mickey stared into

---

*For Fort Wrangel's report of this incident to the War Department, see Appendix.

the shadows of the old carver's shack by the harbor and wondered whether the place was near where Scutdoo's house, the
one knocked down by cannon fire, had stood. Then he thought
about the Natives in 1869 in this place. His brothers. Not so very
long gone from this world, their stories still fresh and still part
of the town and the land. Outside, the rain began to turn to snow.

11

lwood Waters was sipping coffee at the long counter in the cafe portion of the Wrangell Inn's restaurant when Mickey, smacking snow from his jacket, came into the brightly lit room, looked around, saw the little pilot and dropped into the seat next to him. Elwood was between flights. It had been a hard day, snowing and blowing, and he considered he was really earning his pay ferrying loads of freight — which he had to load himself, a job he hated — between the airfield and Everett's logging camp in the boss's big blue De Havilland Beaver amphibian. Perched on his stool, Elwood was flirting with the two young waitresses as they shuffled busily back and forth before his eyes. Elwood's two-tone blue baseball cap with the carefully V'd bill and the gold wing emblem was placed on the varnished wood counter before him. His shirt and jeans were pressed. His lace-up boots were shined carefully.

"What do you think of Shirley?" Elwood

whispered to Mickey, gesturing at one of the girls. "I've about decided I'll marry her — reminds me of the girls in France."

"You were never in France," Mickey said loudly.

"Shhhhh," said Elwood. "Was too in France."

"Yeah?" Mickey was impressed.

Elwood waved his teaspoon around as if he were directing a band. "In the army," he said. "I dabbled in helicopters — and I dabbled in girls." He pointed the spoon at Shirley. "Actually, I am thinking of asking you to marry me," he told the girl, who was taller than Elwood and had a figure, he decided, like a Hollywood starlet. He held up his hand. "It's not a sure thing," he told her. "I'm still thinking about it. There are other candidates. . . ."

The girl gave Elwood a dazzling smile and purposely overflowed his coffee cup so the hot liquid puddled up on the counter. The pilot whipped up his cap a split second before the coffee reached it.

"Lord, she's beautiful," he said to Mickey, bending down to slurp loudly from the rim of the cup. Then, his head still lowered, he looked sideways at Mickey. "You wanna see me?"

"I'd like to go flying," said Mickey.

"Yeah?" said Elwood. "You wanna pay for it? Learn? Ride? What?"

"Just a short ride," said Mickey. "I thought if you were going to fly the Cub some day you'd sort of take me along."

"No pay, huh?"

"Er, well . . ."

"What you wanna go for?" Elwood asked.

"You won't laugh if I tell you?"

"Me?" said Elwood. "Naw."

"You might think it's dumb," persisted Mickey.

"Said I wouldn't laugh, didn't I?" said Elwood. "I promise I won't laugh, I won't — unless it's awfully funny — then, see, I'd hafta laugh."

"I read a legend about a raven. It's a Tlingit story. It's been bothering me. Besides, I want to see Southeastern Alaska from up there. It goes a long way, huh?"

"Long way," said Elwood. "Forever. I ever tell you about when I got lost in the Beaver —" Elwood said suddenly, "What did it do — the raven?"

"Stuck its beak into a cloud and hung there to keep out of a flood."

"Son-of-a-gun," said Elwood, grinning.

"You promised," said Mickey.

"I ain't laughin'," said the little pilot. "It's neat."

Elwood put his cap on carefully, dropped a dollar bill on the counter, saluted Shirley, who waved from the other end of the counter, and rose from his seat. "We'll take the Cub," he told Mickey. "Saturday."

Elwood had an old Piper Cub he used for an occasional student and for forays to Petersburg, Wrangell's closest neighboring town, or to Ketchikan ninety miles south, or the state capital of Juneau, 150 miles north. The boss let him keep the little plane in the corner of the hangar, out of the weather. The Cub's paint was faded, but it was of stout heart and mechanical integrity.

Saturday, Mickey awoke to a cool, windless, cloudy late-winter's day. He struggled into his jeans, boots, wool shirt and down jacket, found his wool watch cap and was at the airport at ten to meet Elwood. Despite his heavy clothing, Mickey shivered — mostly from anticipation. He wanted to see his land from the air. It was important. He was a little afraid of flying like the raven, though, he laughed to himself. He had never been in an airplane.

They rolled the little Cub out of the hangar by hand. Mickey was surprised at how easy it was to push.

"Heck, Elwood," he said, "this thing's made of canvas and pipe." He drummed on the plane's covering with his knuckles and grasped a corner of the plane's fuselage, feeling the tubing structure beneath.

Elwood looked pained. "It's stronger than you think. And it's not canvas. Can't stand people calling it canvas."

"Well, what is it, then?" asked Mickey, running his hand over the plane's faded side. "It feels like canvas. It looks like canvas. And . . ."

"It's linen," grunted Elwood.

Mickey rolled his eyes. "Oh," he said. "Seems to me canvas would be stronger, and . . ."

"Listen, you wanna fly?"

"It looks like awfully strong linen," said the boy.

Following Elwood's check of the machine, they wormed their way aboard, Mickey in front and Elwood tucked into a second seat behind the boy.

The elation that overcame him from the moment the chattering little airplane lifted from the runway into the morning sky shocked Mickey. Eyes glistening and his chest somehow constricted with a strange flow of emotion, the boy watched the straits and islands and mountains fall away and spread out beneath him.

"Jelch," Mickey breathed, "I am here. This is what the raven sees. I am seeing what Jelch the Raven sees."

They floated along over Sumner Strait, passing island after island and then turned slowly and headed east, entering the cleft of the Stikine River where it rolled out from the high coastal range. They followed in minutes the course that would have taken many hours for the old Tlingit traders to navigate up to the first of the river's many glaciers. Mickey saw moose standing as black spots on the white snows of the river flats, easy to find because where the tracks ended there invariably was the moose, standing forlornly in the ice-locked land, or lying down, its long legs tucked awkwardly under it. From the air, finding the moose was an elementary exercise, but from the ground it must have been a monumental task. The river's wooded islands were many. How hard it must have been to come up here with canoes and take moose, Mickey thought.

The boy, in his glassed-in magic carpet, seeing Tlingit lands as none of his forebears had ever seen them, thought then of the legend of how Jelch the Raven escaped a flood that covered the Tlingits' lands by donning a bird-skin jacket and flying high into the sky beyond the reach of the floodwaters. The legend said Raven flew so high he stuck his beak into the clouds and hung there for ten days before the waters subsided and he let go.

The Cub wheeled around lazily and Elwood worked his way out of the river valley and steered toward town across salt water. Mickey turned and shouted over the engine's pop-pop-pop to Elwood:

"How high are those clouds?" The boy pointed upward, through the roof of the airplane.

Elwood leaned forward and spoke into Mickey's ear, "Why?"

"Because, I wonder if we can stick our beak into them." The boy grinned at Elwood.

Elwood wrinkled up his eyes under the bill of his blue

baseball cap with the wings on it. He wore expensive aviator sunglasses that hid his eyes, but Mickey could see the laugh wrinkles out the sides. They extended onto Elwood's cheeks.

The little pilot reached smoothly for the throttle and the engine speeded up. The plane began to climb slowly toward the flat-bottomed, gray cloud layer that hung above them. Suddenly it pierced the clouds and was enveloped in a dark gray vault, void of bearings or substance. As suddenly, Elwood eased the throttle and abruptly lowered the plane's nose, lifting Mickey out of his seat against his seat belt and giving him a queer feeling in the pit of his stomach. The Cub dropped back into the world of light and Mickey could see the islands and the straits stretched out as before. The plane sighed in its gliding descent toward the snow-covered airport far ahead.

Elwood leaned forward. "You mean stick our beak into the clouds like *that*?," he chuckled.

"Yeah," said Mickey. "Just like that!"

The Cub continued dropping from the winter sky, the cold air outside hissing over its wings and around its windows and the little motor gently popping. Mickey, greatly pleased, sat back and watched the airport grow in size.

■ ■ ■

"Hey, you — Klen Nitchkaku."

It was Tim Sipe hailing Mickey from across Main Street. The greeting was insulting, alluding to the Tlingit boy of legend who did not know who he was — "The boy from nowhere."

Mickey ignored the bigger boy, but his heart jumped and he knew this was finally the time.

The fight was brief. When he found himself in the slush

of Main Street the first time, Tim Sipe thought he had slipped. When he rose wet from the street the second time, explosive anger and hurt overtook him and he charged at Mickey. He caught the smaller boy with his shoulder and drove him backward into the corner of a building. But Mickey rode with the thrust and deftly twisted away, grasping Tim's arm in a certain way. After he rose from the slushy gutter the third time, Tim Sipe smacked his soaked cap against his sopping blue jeans and headed out.

"I catch you again, I'll make you darned sorry," he yelled to Mickey. "You watch it, Indian." But Tim knew now he couldn't beat Mickey in a fair fight and would have to resort to ambush. Mickey knew it too.

Editor, who had glimpsed the battle from *The Citizen*, winked as Mickey entered the office.

"Well," said Editor, "you told the truth to me. You didn't hurt him, and he did get wet."

"He'll be back," said Mickey. "It's still a problem. But I have to admit I feel a whole lot better about it all."

Mickey, tasting victory for the first time in his young life, actually felt wonderful. He felt as if he could take care of any problem thrown his way.

Editor motioned toward the back of the office and adjusted his eyeshade. "Ready to go to work, I expect?" he said. "A true warrior is never put off by mere combat. After the battle there is always the paperwork."

"I'm so busy I don't know what I'm doing half the time," said Mickey, taking a seat at the desk. For two days each week Editor had been tutoring Mickey. They had reviewed English, history, mathematics and social studies. They had gone over and over Mickey's textbooks. Editor was teaching the boy to study;

Mickey realized this. He was astounded at the depth of Editor's knowledge and Mickey's head was swimming with it all. He got high C grades, though, on two examinations which, by tradition, he would have flunked outright or cheated his way through, barely passing. At Editor's insistence, Mickey kept his jeans and his shirts and jacket clean and his hair combed. Editor said the neat appearance went with being a scholar and Mickey had laughed.

Editor knew through the grapevine, though, that Mickey still took an alcoholic drink now and then, or a puff, and that the boy's use of colorful language and bad grammar persisted. But all in all Editor was satisfied with the progress they were making.

Aside from Mickey's improvement in school, there was a girl — Julie Powers. She was much in his thoughts lately. Almost at the same time of his improvement in dress and grooming, Mickey noticed Julie noticing him. He caught her staring at him in class one day and, not knowing how else to handle it, he gave her an easy, underhanded wave. She rewarded him with a warm smile that made him feel wonderful — and confused.

Now, though he had not noticed her before, Mickey seemed to glimpse this pretty girl everywhere — in the school halls and library, downtown and even, to his astonishment, in a dream.

He tried to ignore as much as possible this new wrinkle in his life, but it was difficult. Mickey considered asking Julie to a school dance, then rejected the idea. He had never danced, did not socialize with those people, whom he considered "square." Besides, he would probably make a fool of himself if he went to a dance.

Mickey was staring at Editor's office wall thinking of

these developments when he heard the newspaperman talking to him. They were into American history and Editor was trying to elicit a certain date from the boy.

"Huh?" Mickey grunted.

"I was merely attempting to say that it appears we are through for the day," Editor said.

"I went flying," Mickey said.

"Oh — you don't have enough to do already?"

"We're naming the canoe Raven."

Mickey told Editor about the flight. Then he told him about the legend of Raven.

When he had heard, Editor leaned back in his chair across the old desk top from Mickey, folding his hands into a cradle for his head.

"Oh, indeed," Editor said. "I understand perfectly. Raven it certainly must be."

12

hey were in Tom Lincoln's shack. A battered radio blared rock music from a high shelf. Mickey hummed along happily. He was occupied with fashioning a miniature of the canoe. Tom Lincoln left his work on the paddles and edged over to Mickey, peering over the boy's bent back at the model.

"Oops," said the carver, holding a restraining hand out. "You're digging too deep there, my boy. Uncle would have disapproved."

"Geez," said Mickey. "Does it make that much difference?" He held up the model, turning it this way and that. "It looks fine to me."

Tom lifted the chisel from Mickey's hand and gently spun the boy around to face him. "There's a right way and wrong way to do this, Mickey," he said. "I'll show you the right way. Then you'll know."

Tom Lincoln took the little model from Mickey, braced it on the back of the chair, and began taking off thin shavings of cedar. Almost immediately the little hull began to take a much more pleasing form. Mickey shrugged in defeat. Tom handed the wood and the tool back.

"What carving takes is discipline and planning," he told Mickey. "You have to know where you want to go and then you have to go there very carefully. Guess maybe you haven't been too concerned with either of those qualities — discipline and planning — up to now, huh?"

"How would you know?" countered Mickey.

"That's the way it is when you live a dissolute life in a small town," chuckled Tom Lincoln, brushing chips from his wool shirt. "Everybody knows. You get notorious."

"Yeah, well I've changed," the boy said. He went back to work on the model, using the chisel more slowly this time, trying to emulate Tom Lincoln's skillful strokes.

"Not changed enough. Not yet," persisted the carver. "You want to carve in my uncle's shack with my uncle's tools, show some restraint. Take it off thin, work with the grain, give me shavings I can see through."

Mickey's brows wrinkled as he concentrated on the work. "I'm giving this to a girl," he shouted above the music to Tom Lincoln, who had returned to his paddles. Paddles by now were hanging all around the shack. Each had intricate designs carved into the blades. Later they would be painted bright colors so the artwork would flash when the paddlers worked them.

"Which girl's that?"

"Julie Powers. Do you know her?"

"Know her ma. She's working up at the restaurant. Nice. Always smiling."

"That's Julie too," Mickey shouted back, smiling broadly himself.

Julie had been spontaneous and open in choosing Mickey for her friend. She had become his girl by the simple expedient of being physically close to him at school, day after day. That he should begin walking her home followed naturally. It was not a case of her being pushy, either. Their friendship was definitely mutual. Mickey's only worry was that he'd lose her, that his shyness would finally drive her off. Mickey was incapable of the glibness some boys had with girls. His only approach was to be natural, to be Mickey. And he knew that Mickey was sometimes hard to be around.

Mickey was so smitten with the girl that one night he had actually hiked up the hill behind town to face the little house Julie and her mother rented. Across the street from the house, Mickey had leaned against a splintery light pole while rain poured down on him. The light from the pole cast a wet yellow circle on the muddy street before him, the rain blew in a misty veil, and he was soon soaked. After ten minutes of that, Mickey had laughed at himself and, shoulders thrown back and hands thrust deep into his jacket pockets and looking for warmth, walked briskly back down the hill. But he had felt Julie's nearness in the frame house and knowing that she was there, close, represented something important to him. Something of value.

One day after school Mickey and Julie went to the Hang-Out for sodas. At a table they laughed and talked and Mickey almost told her about the canoe. He did tell her about Editor and their studies and how hard it was to change and really begin to study.

"After all," he said, "I'll graduate in May. Then what? I gotta do *something*."

"Like what?" she had asked.

"Like college," Mickey said. The word came out, unexpectedly startling him.

"Oh, where?" Julie asked. "I'm going to the university."

"Oh, there," Mickey replied. "Yep, University of Alaska. I'm studying — ah — history. Especially Native history."

"We'll be together at the university," said Julie. "Won't that be great?"

For a moment Mickey thought he really was changing, that his life was opening up before him. Maybe, he thought, just maybe I could do it.

■ ■ ■

Mickey collected the red, transparent shavings from the model and, cradling them in his palm, took them across the shop to Tom Lincoln. "These good enough?" he asked Tom, who was carving on a paddle and whistling to the terrible radio music.

Tom Lincoln held up the shavings to the light, one by one, and then took the model from Mickey and held it this way and that and ran his fingers over it. He dropped the shavings to the floor and handed the canoe back to Mickey. "Uncle would have smiled," he said, and went back to his own work.

13

lackie sighed along the gunnel of the canoe. The tough Louisianan was not altogether easy with the vessel he had helped to create. It was as if a huge ghost ship had come to his shop from the mysterious, terrifying mists of the archipelago's past. Blackie could easily imagine this very canoe, manned by powerful Tlingit warriors, racing in to take a trading schooner. He could see the blood and hear the screams as men died. Blackie shivered and retreated quickly from the shop, slamming through the greasy door to the front office to find Bob, the taximan, waiting for him anxiously.

"Blackie?" Bob said cautiously. "Now, you're not still mad at me, are you?"

Blackie gave Bob an expansive smile and fell into a chair, motioning his visitor to another.

"Ahhhh, Bob," said Blackie. "C'mon, sit down, have a sody-water." Blackie's eyes narrowed and his thick black brows waggled. He sensed an advantage that would allow him to even the score with Bob.

Six months previously Bob had brought his new Dodge into the shop with ignition problems, which Blackie quickly put right. When it came time to pay, Bob allowed that it was lucky that Dodge was still on warranty.

Blackie had frowned and said, "Don't work on no warranty, Bob. Nope, never."

Bob said, "But, Blackie . . ."

Blackie replied simply, "Nope."

The taximan finally agreed to Blackie's terms — cash. But he left the car at the garage, saying he'd pick it up later.

Bob, watching his chance, came to the shop for his car when Blackie was out with the tow truck. Bob dealt with Blackie's smiling wife, saying, "On warranty. Blackie knows." He left her with a stack of papers.

Blackie returned an hour later, found the Dodge gone and the till no richer, and his little eyes got smaller and his mouth went tight. He sent a spray of tobacco juice into a corner, raised a greasy index finger, and made an imaginary mark in the air. His wife frowned.

Blackie comforted her. "Now, 'taint your fault. Not no-how." Then he sat down to the vexsome work of figuring how to fill out the warranty forms.

Now Bob was back, the garageman smiled faintly at him.

"Doggone, the Dodge is up to Church Street broke down again," said Bob. "Won't move. I think it's the clutch."

"Uh-huh," said Blackie. "Want me to fetch it on down heah?"

Bob nodded. "Warranty's run out. I'll pay cash."

Blackie nodded in understanding and Bob left.

Later, when Bob's sedan was up on the jack in the garage,

Blackie rolled out from under the car, got slowly to his feet, went to his workbench and pawed through a jumble of odds and ends, and came up with a cotter pin, which he held to the light, moistened with his tongue and polished on his greasy smock. Back under the car, Blackie worked a lever, inserted the pin, spread it open, pinching it with pliers for good measure, and grunted his satisfaction. The Dodge was fixed. In ten minutes flat. It was ready to roll. But it didn't.

Blackie stood up, wiped off the Dodge's fender with a rag, patted the car's hood and walked back into his office.

That afternoon Bob appeared.

"Clutch," said Blackie. "You wuz right, Bob."

"Bad?"

"Enough."

"So?"

"Parts," Blackie told him. "Done ordered 'em."

Bob asked how long it would be.

"Oooooh, now," drawled Blackie, holding up two hopelessly greased-stained hands, palms out. "Three, mebbe four days to get the parts up heah. A day to get 'em in. Say five, six days — a week."

Bob groaned and went around to the shop and looked at his taxi up on blocks, then went away, shaking his head.

A week later, Bob was still waiting. "Gee, Blackie," he wailed. "This is costing me money."

"Uh-huh," said Blackie. "Parts ain't here yet, but they're coming."

At nine days, Blackie phoned Bob. "Done," he told the taximan.

When Bob showed up, Blackie handed him a bill, and Bob got out his money and began carefully counting it out.

Blackie followed each bill with his eyes, his lips moving as he kept count.

"Hundred twenty, hundred thirty, hundred forty-five," said Bob. "Why Blackie, that's exactly what that warranty job came to."

"What a coinceedence," mused Blackie. He took Bob's money and dropped it into the cash drawer, shoving the drawer shut with a bang.

When Blackie related the story to Tom Lincoln as they worked that night, Tom listened with an appreciation for Blackie's business acumen.

"I take it," he said, "the warranty money hasn't come in yet?"

"Nope," said Blackie. "That always takes a while, you know."

"Blackie, I like the story fine," said Tom Lincoln. "But I wonder, when that money does come in, what will you do with it?"

Blackie's eyebrows shot up. "Well, keep it, a-course," he said. "Put it right here in this-here billfold." He pulled out his outsized worn leather purse, which he kept secured to his trousers with a massive brass chain. Blackie did all his business from the billfold; he didn't believe in banks and he believed only marginally in taxes.

"That's dishonest, isn't it?" asked Tom Lincoln.

Blackie rubbed his chin and stared at the carver. "Not where I come from, it ain't. Man does something like Bob did — sneaky thing — why you gotta act. Cain't just sit there and get took."

Tom Lincoln nodded. He'd known Blackie a good many years and he grasped that the garageman's sense of justice, if it wasn't entirely square according to conventional philosophies, made a lot of sense — for a Louisiana man.

14

ickey was on Muir Mountain again. Alone, he had climbed to look out over the town and to think about his life, which was becoming more complicated than ever he imagined it could.

The boy sat in a clearing and looked down at the houses and stores of town and at the harbor beyond. He could see, just below him, a streetlamp which, not many months before, he had dispatched with a rock just for the devilment of it. Where had that other Mickey Church gone? Things were so different now.

Wrangell painted a pretty picture below, perched around the north end of the island and fronting the little bay where fishing boats nosed neatly into their slips or rafted two and three deep at the floats. The town's frame houses, steep-roofed and angular, were mostly well kept and the few painted in bright hues instead of the standard white or gray made warm splashes of color. Wooden walkways, holdovers from the days when Wrangell was growing in no-street, slapdash fashion up the marshy hillsides, served as pedestrian links and seemed to tie the houses together. Moss in the roof gutters and on roofs shone soft green. The town looked serene and secure as it went about its business this early spring day.

How different Wrangell appeared to the musing boy from the Wrangell the naturalist John Muir saw when he stepped from a little steamer to the muddy shore in July of 1879. Mickey had read about that first visit by Muir to the outpost. The naturalist called Wrangell a place of "devil-may-care abandon," with its mud and muck and makeshift houses and tree stumps growing in the boggy streets.

Mickey sighed and looked again at his neat and tidy town. Wisps of wood smoke floated lazily. A slight breeze rippled the waters of Zimovia Strait. A floatplane droned in, alighted offshore, and made for the harbor.

In the months after John Muir's arrival, Mickey knew, he had come to know Wrangell as no other visitor had ever been able to. The great naturalist roamed the town, met everyone, and even hired a canoe for an eight-hundred-mile voyage of exploration, which took him through the archipelago far to the north to Glacier Bay. In fact, Muir was the first white man ever known to visit that many-glaciered wonder.

John Muir, Mickey thought, would have liked the canoe we are building. How much is it like the one he traveled in? He would have liked me sitting here, too — on his mountain.

Mickey moved higher up the slope and deeper into the trees, trying to imagine just where Muir might have built his famous bonfire that made flames soar into the nighttime storm, so Muir imagined they touched the bases of the racing clouds.

Mickey wondered whether Scutdoo might have come to this very place on the mountain, alone, frightened and hunted.

How many Native boys have come up here through the centuries to think, like I am doing, he mused, as he stared off through the thick trees. The sounds of town did not penetrate here. He was surrounded by the age-old forest. Ravens clicked and called nearby and a breeze sprang up, felt its way through the timber and rustled the boughs above him.

It was then, thinking of the death of old Scutdoo, of the ancient hill, of his people, that Mickey remembered the cemetery and felt remorse. He saw the topped gravestones again, and the remains of the carefully fabricated grave fences, and remembered how it had meant nothing that summer night to rampage through that place which, after all, was far-gone through neglect and decades of weather.

Suddenly a thought struck him. Mickey left the mountain and gained the streets of town in ten minutes' fast walking. He went straight to the newspaper office.

"I want you to come somewhere with me," Mickey told Editor.

Editor looked puzzled.

"To a cemetery. I helped wreck it once and I want you to see it, that's all."

■ ■ ■

Editor eased his old truck from the main highway, negotiated a steep, graveled incline, splashed through a deep rain puddle and finally brought the truck to a halt halfway into a stand of giant, ancient trees.

The old Native graveyard lay before them. Mossy-trunked

spruce and hemlock trees crowded close together. Under them it was dark, cool and moist. Editor and Mickey made their way in. There was an awful hush. Spongy ground was underfoot. It was uneven, ridged and holed and torn as if a battle had been fought there. Graves left unattended for decades had sunk, casting their outlines in the ground. The gravestones had almost all fallen over. They glowed flatly white against the dull green-brown of the earth. There were remnants of grave houses and grave fences. Beer cans, paper and other refuse lay everywhere.

"How much of this ruin did you and your rowdy friends account for?" Editor asked Mickey.

"It's been like this forever," Mickey said. "All we did was kick a few fences down and push over some gravestones. You know."

"Nice boys," Editor said.

"I know," the boy replied grimly, picking up part of a grave fence and dropping it carefully in with the remains of its brothers. "Then, I was different. Do you suppose this could be fixed up? I mean, these *are* people. It all seems so wrong for them just to be forgotten this way."

"Some very good people here, too, no doubt," said Editor. "It might be fixed up. The question is, why has it been forgotten in the first place?"

Editor moved away absently, pushing into the under-growth, and Mickey followed, being careful not to be caught by whipping branches.

Half an hour later, in a little clearing in the trees, they came upon a square gravestone lying alone with no sign of a grave at all. Editor rolled the stained white stone over and hunkered to squint at the weathered inscription. He read slowly aloud:

DAVID TOWAATT
A Chief of the
STICKINE TRIBE
Killed by the
HOOTZNOO INDIANS
Jan. 15, 1880
AGED ABOUT 65 YEARS
He believed in the Savior

Editor got to his feet. "My word," he said. "We have found a famous fellow. We have found a famous fellow indeed. And a hero as well. And a statesman. My word."

Editor squatted again before the stone, his face a study, tracing the inscription with a finger. Finally he rose and, hands on his hips, faced around and gazed past the gravel beach and across the surface of Zimovia Strait at the looming mass of Woronkofski Island. The snow on the island was now a mere dusting on the upper reaches, a cool gray veil on the high timber. At the very summits, though, the winter snow held on, smooth and deep and gleaming.

"This place is a disgrace," Editor finally said suddenly, turning back to the ruin around him. "And this forgotten stone is that of a leading figure in recent Tlingit history. Towaatt was a fine leader, a hero, and look at this." Editor gestured at the stone. "Just look."

Mickey knew about the Native hero, too, from Tom Lincoln and from his history class.

"Towaatt tried to keep the army from shelling the village in 1869," he said. "He was a sub-chief or something like that, under Chief Shakes. He tried to calm Shakes down when Shakes wanted to fight. There was a village on

Etolin Island that Towaatt ran, too."

"That isn't all," Editor said. "He was John Muir's canoe captain when Muir took his famous Glacier Bay voyage. Mr. Muir had plenty to say about Towaatt, and it was all good."

■ ■ ■

The gaunt Boston man wanted to see ice mountains — at the beginning of winter!

Towaatt thought it was mad, but John Muir seemed anything but mad. He seemed a strong individual, not so different from Native adventurers. And the Rev. S. Hall Young — well, that one was a true friend who had brought Towaatt to his savior. And Mr. Young was going along on the trip.

Towaatt finally agreed to provide his canoe and to captain it. Besides Towaatt, Mr. Young and Muir, three other Natives were going — Kadachan, a Chilkat, and John, and Sitka Charley.

So it was that they set off westward along Sumner Strait, departing late in the afternoon of October 14, 1879, to the wailings and predictions of doom delivered by wives and others who were certain that if a storm did not drown them, hostile Natives would simply murder the travelers.

But the voyage was successfully carried out and Muir gave Towaatt most of the credit.

Not many weeks after Towaatt returned his passengers to Wrangell, the old Native was obliged to arbitrate a confrontation between Wrangell Tlingits and visiting Hootznoo Indians. Towaatt shooed his friend Mr. Young inside the fort, out of possible harm, and went unarmed at the head of his young men to meet the enemy. Towaatt fell dead at the first hostile volley.

■ ■ ■

"You know what John Muir wrote about Towaatt when Towaatt was killed?" Mickey asked Editor.

"What, Lad?" said Editor.

Mickey put one foot up onto a tree stump, held his arms wide for theatrical effect, and quoted: "Thus died for his people the noblest old Roman of them all."

"How did you know that?" Editor asked, impressed.

"I read," said Mickey. "I read."

■ ■ ■

They were back at *The Citizen* office.

"How can Towaatt's gravestone be left like that?" asked Mickey. "And how can he be forgotten? Hardly anyone even knows about Towaatt, but he's sort of to Wrangell what President Lincoln was to the country, isn't he?"

"As Dead-eye Dick once proclaimed, Lad — it's a queer world," Editor replied.

"Yeah," said Mickey thoughtfully. "Well, I'm finding out why this cemetery is abandoned."

"Careful, Lad," replied Editor, leaning back so his old swivel chair squeaked and groaned beneath him. "You may not be ready for what you learn."

Mickey eyed Editor curiously and went out.

owaatt?" said Mrs. Hackett, kneading her wrinkled brown brow and staring at Mickey with eyes magnified by thick glasses. "No, I don't know 'em."

"He's been dead a long time," Mickey told her. "You wouldn't have known him, but I thought you might have heard of him when you were little. Did you?"

"Didn't know 'em," said Mrs. Hackett.

"Do you know about the Native graveyard out at the point, then?" Mickey pointed toward Cemetery Point.

"Haven't seen that place in years," said Mrs. Hackett. "Not in a lot of years. Lots of our people buried out there, though." Then, clutching a well-used paper bag in which she carried her mail each day, Mrs. Hackett turned and shuffled away toward the post office, leaving Mickey on Main Street.

He had talked to three Natives so far and none had known of the hero Towaatt. All knew about the graveyard but none seemed to care that it was untended — virtually in ruins.

Now, nearly late for class after lunch hour, Mickey sprinted through alleys and across yards and burst into the school building just under the wire. He'd skipped his lunch to research his extra-credit history paper on the burial ground and Towaatt, and had gotten exactly nowhere. "Well, not nowhere," Mickey thought as he hurried up the crowded, ancient stairs to the second floor, and class. "At least I found out our history's being lost and nobody seems to care about the cemetery." Editor hadn't been anywhere near right. So far Mickey could easily handle the little he had learned.

Next day Mickey sprinted from the school on the lunch bell, ran arms flailing for balance down the wet, grassy hill, across Main Street, and on to city hall. He was just in time to catch Mr. Puffin, the city manager, on his way to the market to buy his sandwich.

"Sure, I'll talk to you, Mickey," said the portly official. "Just let me get my lunch over at Benjamin's Market first. Then we'll have a meeting on that bench over there. Lucky no rain, huh?"

The pair sat on the bench, the large, kindly-eyed man in his wrinkled brown suit, a paper towel over his lap to catch crumbs from his lunch, and the Native boy, poised carefully over a small notepad. Their bench overlooked Zimovia Strait. Crows and ravens and gulls hovered or strutted on the grass nearby, all eyeing the man's food.

"There was a Native cemetery over on Shustak Point," said Mr. Puffin, indicating the timbered spit of land across the bay. On the point were fish docks, fuel tanks and a great many houses. "But the burial ground was on private property, see, and it isn't there anymore. The owners of the land decided to build there. I don't know what happened to the gravestones."

"How could a Native burial ground be on private property?" asked Mickey innocently. "Wasn't it there first?"

The official smiled at the boy.

"Oh, I don't know. It just was property belonged to old man Smith, and he elected to build there. Came over to the city and got a permit and up went a couple of houses.

"I'll tell you, Mickey. The city offered to move the graves but the Natives, you know, told us hands off. We weren't insensitive to the historical significance over there — no sir. But we couldn't touch the place unless the Natives said so, and they said no, so nothing was done."

"Which Natives?" asked Mickey.

"Oh, I don't remember," said Mr. Puffin. "Just town Natives. A committee, I think. Or something."

"You ever hear of a Native chief named Towaatt, Mr. Puffin?"

The official took a bite of sandwich, shifted the morsel so it puffed out one cheek, and spoke past it.

"Happens I know a little history, Mickey. Your man Towaatt was John Muir's canoe captain. When Muir went up and discovered Glacier Bay more than a hundred years ago, Towaatt was the canoe captain.

"And according to what I've read, Towaatt was buried on that point over there." Mr. Puffin pointed across the bay. "Is that what you're getting at?"

Mickey had found the same information in one history book, but only one, and he still wasn't sure what he suspected was true, but it was beginning to look true. He turned to face the city official.

"Then how come Towaatt's gravestone is at the burial ground out by the park?" he asked the official.

"Is it?" said Mr. Puffin. "Don't know. You tell me."

"Someone wanted the Shustak Point gravestones out of the way. They loaded them into a truck and took them to the old burial ground and just dumped them." Mickey looked at Mr. Puffin. "It seems to me that's what happened, and I think that was a bad thing to do."

Mr. Puffin chewed silently. Finally he said: "It wasn't the city, if that is what happened, Mickey. I agree, if that is the way of it, it was a bad thing to do. One time I really tried to get something started in regards to the burial ground on the point there, to move the graves in a dignified way. It was real frustrating. Couldn't get any cooperation. No one seemed to care at all."

"I want to know where Towaatt was buried," said the boy. "It's important to me. Has the city got any records of burials?"

"Not that far back, I'm afraid." Mr. Puffin pushed his last cookie into his mouth, wadded up his papers, tossed them expertly into a "Keep Wrangell Tidy" trash can, and rose. "Well, back to the old grind," he said. "That's all I can tell you. See me anytime." He ambled away toward his office.

Mickey stayed, gazing across the strait at Woronkofski Island, which brooded under a cover of gentle clouds.

"Towaatt," the boy said quietly to himself. "Somebody cares. *I* care."

Mickey had time for one more quick visit before he was due back in class, so he headed for the building supply store owned by Ernie Gates and found Gates stirring the contents of a small box on his counter.

"Fishing flies," said Gates. "Not so many people use them around the island, but I do. They work pretty good. I'm looking for a little yellow and black fellow, never misses this time of year."

Mr. Gates looked at the box in perplexity. "Can't see so well anymore, Mickey. Would you take a look for me?"

Mickey stirred the flies around and found a likely candidate. He held it up.

"Almost," said the building supply man. "But that's not the one. Do you mind looking a little more?"

Mickey searched and asked his questions. Mr. Gates listened and stared down with patient, grandfatherly eyes as the young Native unfolded his story and told about his concerns for the burial ground and for Tlingit culture.

Mickey found another fly and held it up. Mr. Gates nodded, hooked the fly in his cap, and put the box away under the counter.

Then the Native building supply man rested his elbows on the counter top and motioned Mickey closer. The shop was silent and smelled of cut lumber, paint and age. A timber creaked somewhere as someone moved about in the apartment upstairs.

"Towaatt is gone," said Mr. Gates softly. "Chief Shakes is no more. Natives are not paddling canoes anymore — they are not found on the waters or on the beaches as in the past. Natives stopped carving totem poles — poles that meant anything, anyway — long ago. Did you know that? Native boys don't run on the beach and swim naked in the winter and beat each other with sticks to get strong for battle any longer. . . ."

Mr. Gates paused, holding out his arms dramatically. His kindly, broad face and white hair made him look like a chief himself.

"Where did it all go, Mickey? Read your history. Have your heroes. See Wrangell in your mind as it was, and be proud of your past. Be proud to be a Tlingit. But that's all. Don't fret about it."

Mickey stared at the man who had been a city councilman, a leader of his people, and started to speak, but Mr. Gates held up a restraining hand.

"You're Native, Mickey. But you have been born wholly into a white culture. Bless you, boy, you think like a white man with your brain, but you feel as a Native with your heart. Poor boy. You'll have to sort it out. I did. At least most of the time I believe I did. Learn, Mickey. Study, get educated. That will give you the stuff it takes to get beyond this hurt you're feeling."

The building supply man dug at his eyes with his brown knuckles, then he began sorting through a stack of flimsy receipts and said to Mickey: "Gotta get back to work. And you have to get back to school. That's where you'll find what we're both looking for, I think."

Mickey left, ambling across Main Street and absently greeting friends from school. He cut between two buildings and climbed the grassy hill. At the top, in front of the old school building, he turned and looked once more across the strait to Woronkofski Island. He had decided for himself that that was "Towaatt's Island." A rain shower was moving along the far-off beach, dousing the timber and blackening the sea.

"Natives are not paddling canoes anymore — they are never found on the waters or on the beaches," Mr. Gates had said. Mickey grimaced, smiled, shrugged, turned away from the scene and took the schoolhouse steps three at a time.

16

t was late in May and the canoe was all but finished. It brooded in the dimness of the shop, still a secret from all except Mickey, Blackie, Tom, Editor and Blackie's wife. It was thirty feet long and seven wide. Blackie and Tom had built in wooden thwarts for strength and as seats for twenty paddlers. The beautiful yellow cedar paddles were finished and placed carefully inside the hull, awaiting the great day of launching.

The bow of the canoe was thrust out haughtily where it would ride high over the water and well forward of the vessel's sharp cutwater. The symmetry of the hull showed startlingly fine even in the diffused light of the old shop.

"We done her," said Blackie, as he and Mickey lounged against the battered workbench. They had been leaning and looking silently for a full five minutes.

"I'll tell you, Mickey," Blackie continued.

"Them Natives, now, they was real artists. This is one beautiful boat here."

"How many hours do you suppose we've got in her?" asked Mickey.

"Ohhhh, now," drawled Blackie. "Thousand mebbe. We all been workin' our shifts right regular — even you, even with all your love affairs and studies and such."

"Not love affairs, Blackie," said Mickey, coloring slightly. "I have one girl — Julie. You know that."

He and Julie were more or less steadies now, spending more and more of their leisure time together. As their closeness grew, Mickey came near on several occasions to telling the girl about the canoe, but he had not done so.

As if reading Mickey's mind, Blackie said, "I reckon you'll be a-tellin' little Julie about this-here canoe purty soon, huh? If you haven't a-ready."

"Nope, not anyone, Blackie. That was our agreement. Have you? Told anyone?"

Blackie peered at Mickey intently. "What's that?" he said, cupping an ear. "Ah didn't hear dat?"

"Sorry," said Mickey, smiling.

"Uh," grunted the garageman. "Old Blackie he don't go back on his word — never. Not with his friends, no-how."

"I know that, Blackie. You never do."

Blackie suddenly became solemn. He looked at his dirty square hands, first at the backs, then at the palms, studying them carefully. Then he thrust them into the pockets of his once white but now grimy shop smock.

"I gotta tell you something," Blackie said to the boy.

Mickey looked up. "What?"

"Old Blackie, he's a-dyin'," Blackie said softly.

"Oh," Mickey said. "What did you say?"

"Dyin'. I'm a-dyin'," Blackie repeated carefully. "Doc Coulter says I am, so I guess that's right. I had tests. Came out no good. Got somethin' inside me, right here. . . ." Blackie held a hand to his side. "It's killin' me — quick, too."

Mickey started to speak but Blackie stopped him with a gesture.

"Lived a lot of times when I shoulda been dead," he said. "I been lucky — to right now." Blackie leaned so close to the boy that Mickey could see individual black whiskers against the garageman's brown chin. "Say, don't let that wife of mine bury me on the island. Can't stand the thought of that rain comin' in on me, and that cold ground. I want to go home, home to Louisiana, hear?" Blackie shuddered. His square shoulders seemed to droop under the grimy smock. Then, with an effort, he straightened and stared through the dimness at the boy.

Mickey peered back into Blackie's dark eyes.

"No!" Mickey half cried. Then the boy hurled himself against Blackie, clasping the garageman with all his strength. The two rocked in embrace close by the high hull of the canoe.

"Sheeesh," crooned Blackie, mussing the boy's hair roughly. "It's true, Mickey. But think of it this-a-way — they's worse things in life than a-dyin'. I know."

"You don't look sick," said Mickey, his voice muffled. "Maybe Doc Coulter is wrong."

"Naw," said Blackie. "Couple of months, he says, and Ole Blackie's gone."

Blackie pushed Mickey gently away. "Say," he said, "did I ever tell you about the time this-here new transport plane — a purty two-engine thing, double-decker, it was — come along to England for us paratroop guys to ride in?

"They wanted to know if a jumper'd hit the tail. Now, how come them brilliant engineers hadn't figured that one out a-ready? Ohhhh, my, I don't know. Me and a couple of other crazies went up and just jumped on out with all our gear on — guns and knives and bombs and stuff. We went straight down — whoosh. Didn't come nowhere near the tail of that thing.

"Then there was this-here trip we made when we come back with a French washing machine and three bicycles — stole 'em all on the run. We just made it back for our meet with the airplane takin' us on outta there — my, they was German sodjers everywhere — and when we threw all that loot on and climbed in after it, they thought we was crazy. My, we was bad and tough in those days, yessir, we was that. . . ." Blackie laughed and his eyes twinkled.

In the following days, he continued working on his cars and on the canoe, which seemed to demand never-ending finishing touches thought up by Blackie and Tom Lincoln. The canoe was more stately, haughty and mysterious than ever, hidden away behind the garage partition. Blackie built a heavy wooden slide to extend out and down from the garage's back door for the launching.

"You just grease her up," he told Mickey and Tom one day, "and wait for that high tide. Then pull her onto the slide with the little winch. When she's a-teeterin' give her a big shove. Down she'll go, slicker'n you'd believe."

"You'll be here to do it yourself," said Mickey.

"Nope," said Blackie simply. "Ole Blackie won't be."

And so it was that one day Blackie closed the shop door for the last time, climbed into his battered green tow truck and drove alone to the hospital to check himself in.

Three days later he died.

Editor and Mickey and Tom Lincoln were there with him, along with Blackie's wife, who sat in a corner of the hospital room and stared sightlessly straight ahead.

"Blackie said he wanted to be buried in Louisiana," Mickey said to her quietly.

She nodded and smiled up at Mickey. "All right," she said. "I know."

Two days later, Mickey saw the garageman off on his last flight and remembered what Blackie had told him about the parachute jump in England, and about all the other adventures the old soldier had confided to him.

"I'll bet he'd even jump out of that thing," Mickey thought, as they loaded the coffin into the belly of the big jet. "If they asked him to, he'd do it. He was so brave. I wonder what the pilots would think if they knew they had a man like Blackie with them. Why, Blackie's the best man on that airplane."

Mickey stayed to watch the jet roar away in a curving climb. He watched it out of sight and then took the asphalt road up the hill away from the airport toward town, walking slowly.

Suddenly, at the top of the first hill, Mickey darted off the pavement, leaped a roadside ditch, and plunged into the forest beyond. He sprinted between trees, hurdling fallen logs and leaping across and splashing through muskeg puddles.

Far away from the road sounds, Mickey stopped, gasping for breath and sobbing. He stayed in the wilderness of the timber and muskeg for a long while. When he finally came out, he was composed and he took to the asphalt again, walking ramrod straight, and made his way to town.

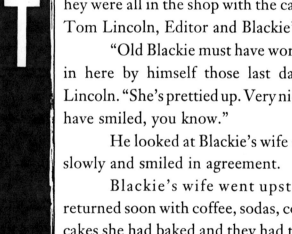

hey were all in the shop with the canoe — Mickey, Tom Lincoln, Editor and Blackie's wife.

"Old Blackie must have worked pretty hard in here by himself those last days," said Tom Lincoln. "She's prettied up. Very nice. Uncle would have smiled, you know."

He looked at Blackie's wife and she nodded slowly and smiled in agreement.

Blackie's wife went upstairs then, and returned soon with coffee, sodas, cookies and little cakes she had baked and they had their "wake" for Blackie, though none of them admitted outright that it was what it was.

They reminisced about Blackie, and Mickey repeated the stories Blackie had told him at the last.

"Blackie, he did a lot over there in the war," his wife said. "He was pretty brave, you know. He didn't say much, except sometimes to joke. Lots of medals upstairs."

"What will you do now?" Mickey asked her. "I mean, are you going to stay right here and run this place?"

"Yes, for now," she replied. "It will be different for me. But for now, yes. I can't fix cars," she said. "Oh, maybe I can fix 'em like Bob's Dodge." Her eyes twinkled and Tom Lincoln, who was privy to the joke, laughed.

They inspected the canoe again, counted the paddles and reviewed the launching instructions, and proclaimed all in readiness.

"Let's keep her sprayed down and pour some water in the bottom," said Tom Lincoln. "Don't want her splitting open on us."

Mickey sighted along the canoe, moved around the shop trying to get as far away from the clutter as he could so he could see the vessel's lines. He was startled by its resemblance to the dream canoe he had seen racing along the shore at the old village site.

"A month," Mickey thought. "School's out, the canoe's finished and I have a month and a little more before the Fourth of July. Then summer, then the university, Julie, a job, the future . . ."

Suddenly a line of old John Muir's occurred to the boy. With Wrangell in sight at long last at the end of the colossal round-trip canoe voyage through Southeastern Alaska, the Rev. Mr. Young had been elated about their finally getting back to civilization. Muir had not joined him in his elation, commenting to the minister that surely there was no news in town worth knowing compared to that they had learned from the wilderness.

Mickey, a Tlingit boy, had seldom been outside the town, into that wilderness, and the truth of it loomed, to the boy, as large as the canoe in the confines of Blackie's shop.

Suddenly he knew what he would do with that month — the next four weeks.

18

ickey was searching along the harbor float for a certain scow. When he came to it he stepped aboard, found a dry spot, and sat down to wait. It was misting rain but the lacy veils didn't seem to be too wet. Mickey watched the harbor scene contentedly.

Soon, Hank Hudson came whistling down from the dock above and headed for the scow through the rain. He had a grocery box on each shoulder and was trailed by another man, who carried two more boxes. Hank's dog trailed the two of them at a distance, dragging his frayed leash behind him.

The trapper showed no surprise on finding Mickey in his boat, but began handing the groceries in for the boy to stow. The dog jumped into the scow and tried to work his way under Mickey's arms for patting, interfering with the stowing.

"He's taken a liking to you," said Hank.

"That's a fact, and a strange one. Ole Chinook, he don't like strangers that much — sometimes not at all." He chuckled.

When the loading of supplies was complete, Hank Hudson looked at Mickey as if he had just seen him.

"Well," he asked the boy. "Comin' or stayin'?"

"Can I?" said Mickey.

"Asked ya, didn't I? Where's your gear?" Hank Hudson looked around the interior of the scow.

"Up on the dock," admitted Mickey. "I was hoping, see . . ."

"Well, blazes, Boy," snapped Hank Hudson. "Go get it. We ain't got all blamed day. It's gettin' late."

The old man, the boy and the dog moved out of Wrangell Harbor in the scow, southwest-bound, in the rain. Mickey rode in the bow of the boat, Chinook nestled tightly under his arm. Hank Hudson, his worn Stetson hat pulled down tightly against the wind, sprawled in the stern and steered. The old man smiled broadly at the sight of the boy and the dog.

No sooner had Wrangell faded into the mist astern than Mickey knew for certain he was right in doing this — going off with Hank Hudson. They straight-arrowed ahead, flanked by timbered mountainsides plunging to salt water. The near horizon was enveloped in mist and the distances beckoned the boy and the man on and on, enfolding them in veil after comforting veil of warm rain.

They ran for an hour — two. Salt spray flew, the scow sped over a small chop with a *phutt-phutt-phutt* rhythm so regular that Mickey composed a little tune and hummed it in time. The dog sat with his nose above the boat's rail, taking the measure of the sea and the land. Essence of gull and seal and salt and weed and trees and the delicious odor of dead things,

Chinook took in through his shiny muzzle and toted up in his brain. He took exquisite pleasure in his work.

As they passed close by a rocky point, the dog's ears perked sharply and he looked back at Hank Hudson, who immediately closed the throttle on the outboard motor. The scow came down from on top of the water like a thing shot, and wallowed in the wave that overtook it. They idled toward a half-moon-shaped gravel beach and the boat finally crunched gently ashore.

Hank Hudson reached for his rifle case. He pulled the weapon from it, placed the gun on a thwart, and with an easy wave of his arm, motioned the now quivering Chinook out of the scow. The dog's muscles coiled under Mickey's hand and Chinook launched himself with a restrained, excited *whoof* onto the gravel, dived straight into the underbrush and disappeared.

The old man stood, poled the boat off, started the kicker mounted alongside the scow's big motor, and began to cruise slowly along close to the shore. The motor thump-thumped, the rain slanted against Mickey's face. The boy turned and held his arms out in a question to Hank Hudson, who beamed at him and made eating motions. Mickey nodded, understanding, and turned back to watch the woods as they slid by.

Ten minutes later there was a furious barking ashore and a buck deer bolted onto the beach just opposite the scow. Hank Hudson took up the rifle calmly and shot the animal once. It crumpled up on the beach and was still. It happened in a twinkling. Chinook exploded from the trees then, seconds behind the fleeing animal, sniffed at it and sat down next to it, panting and watching the approaching scow.

"Chinook's a great hunter," said the old man. He motioned with his arm and the dog, his official duties over, got up and began trotting along the beach, his nose to the gravel.

"Isn't it illegal or something, shooting that deer? You got a license for that, Hank?"

"Illegal? What's that?" said Hank Hudson, putting his rifle away in its case but leaving it close by the body of the deer. "Oh, some say so. Actually, we take a deer when we're hungry, just like the Tlingits used to do. I'm hungry, Mickey. Ain't you?"

Mickey nodded, "But . . ."

"You see anything wrong with old Hank and Mickey eating that-there deer?" Hank Hudson had his knife out and was preparing to clean the animal.

"What deer?" asked Mickey, kneeling close to watch and to learn.

They entered Hank Hudson's pass just at dusk, ducking out of a windy and rough Clarence Strait, and found the trapper's floathouse cold and damp but secure. The old man had a fire going quickly and soon the place was cheery and warm.

"Home, sweet home," said Hank Hudson, lighting his pipe. "I love this broken-down old joint, I sure do."

"Me too," said Mickey, squatting and feeling the warmth from the cast-iron stove Hank Hudson had stuffed with wood chips. The old cabin was built on a float of huge logs strung tightly together with chain and cables and anchored in the center of the pass. Huge old trees surrounded the pass and protected the place from the high southerly winds that could shriek and howl in this part of the archipelago. The snug cabin did seem familiar and homelike to the boy. He looked forward to the morning when he could explore.

In the days that followed, Mickey learned to collect wild rice and mushrooms, to catch and smoke fish, to smoke deer meat, and to eat the giant oatmeal cookies the old man turned out by the stack on his cast-iron wood stove and called "horse-power."

On the eighth day Mickey saved Hank Hudson's life and nearly died himself — of fright.

They were out after a goat, high on a mountain above the pass. They had climbed hard all morning, first through high grass, then heavy timber, then through thinning copses of trees, until they emerged onto rock and gravel high up. They could see from this giddy altitude far across the islands and waters. The islands marched in somnolent precision through glittering channels. Lakes winked on many of the high meadows. Hank Hudson pointed with the barrel of his rifle for Mickey to see how most of the land tended north and south.

"Ice," said Hank Hudson. "It moved along and carved all this. It traveled from north to south advancing, and from south to north retreating. Grinding away for centuries."

"I see places that don't look north and south to me," Mickey challenged. "Canyons and stuff."

"You do, huh?" said Hank Hudson. "Well, me too, but mostly it's the way I say. Sometimes there were local hold-ups, see? Side valleys and such where the ice had to do little detours to get back to its main direction. That's what you're seeing."

"Hank," said Mickey, leaning his own rifle carefully against a rock, mindful of the precautions the old man had been drilling into him every day about handling guns. "How come you know so much about it?"

"I can read!" snapped Hank Hudson. "About everything you want to know is in a book somewhere. Some real smart people have written down what they know — all you have to do is look."

The old man chuckled. "Of course, so have some real

dumb ones — written books, I mean. Trick is to know one from the other."

Mickey peered at Hank Hudson, who squinted back at the boy from beneath his old Stetson. Hank reached into his mouth, pulled out his upper teeth, examined them against the sky, pursed his now caved-in mouth, and spit clumsily. He slipped his teeth back in and clicked them at Mickey.

"Gross," said the boy. The old man grinned and set out again toward the top of the peak. The summit was near, just over a rocky shoulder ahead.

Mickey had found it hard to keep pace with Hank Hudson's graceful, surefooted, ground-eating stride. The boy was determined, though, and although he actually had to run to close gaps, he never called for a halt or let on that he was suffering. Hank Hudson knew, though, and he smiled at the tenacity of the boy. "Tlingits is tough customers," Hank Hudson said to himself. "Even if they are town-born and -raised — just naturally tough customers."

When the old man strode around the last rock face standing between him and the backbone of the mountain, he knew then that he was dead.

A brown bear, eight feet tall and as wide as a small truck, loomed before him. It was not a place where a bear ought to be, but there it was. When the bear saw Hank Hudson blunder around the rocks, it was startled and then outraged. It stood to its full height, whoofed, and then dropped and charged from a distance of fifteen yards. The old man raised his rifle and pumped a cartridge into the chamber in one motion, but in that flash of a second he knew it was too late. This colossal bear would tear him open or swat him dead before he could fire.

Blam! Blam! The explosions were at Hank Hudson's ear.

In that space of time he thought the bear had hit him and that it was the shock of the death blow he was experiencing.

The big grizzly staggered, veered to one side, ran full tilt off the ridge, and tumbled over and over down the sheer face of the mountain. Finally it disappeared in an explosion of dislodged rocks and broken brush and trees far, far below them. It had come within a foot of the old man, so close the air was fanned by the passing of the huge body and Hank Hudson smelled live bear smell as close as he'd ever want to smell it.

Hank Hudson turned to find Mickey close behind him, down on one knee. The boy's rifle barrel was still smoking, and Mickey himself was staring vacantly.

"Geez," the boy said. "Man! I never want to go through anything like that again."

"Second time's easier," said Hank Hudson casually, fishing for his pipe and tobacco and rigging up to smoke. But when he tried to light up, his hand shook so that he threw the match away. "You got a shell under that hammer?" he asked.

Mickey shrugged. "I don't know."

"Tarnation, boy," scolded the old man. "Lever her back there, carefully, and see, 'fore you shoot one of us. You bein' some kind of an expert bear-killer and all, I'd expect you to know if your blamed gun's ready to shoot or not. Fix her up like I taught you."

Mickey, still kneeling, looked up at Hank Hudson. "Hank," he said, "is it smart to go barging around corners like that in bear country?"

The trapper finally succeeded in lighting his pipe. He blew out a rich cloud of blue smoke.

"Nope," Hank Hudson replied. "And don't you forget it as long as you live. I'm an old fool, and that's a fact.

"And that was some shootin'. How'd you manage to miss old Hank and hit that-there bear?"

"Beats me," said Mickey. "I had my eyes closed."

The old man's eyes widened. Then he began to laugh and the boy laughed with him. Their laughter boomed across the ridge and echoed into the age-old canyons on the desolate mountain. And Mickey Church felt like a man for the first time in his young life.

19

A week later, Mickey, Hank Hudson and the dog Chinook were off after king salmon. They ran with poles rigged out from the scow, lived from stores kept under a tarpaulin, and slept on the boat's floorboards or in a camp on the beach. They smelled of fish and their hands were stained, their clothing stiff with dried fish slime. Their rain gear was smeared with fish oil until it glistened and shone. They were piling their salmon up in the scow and selling it to a cannery tender. It was a wonderful life. Mickey was absorbing so many experiences through these days that he felt dizzy and full up.

"Hank, how long have you lived like this?" Mickey asked the old man as they gutted fish and hurled them, glistening, into the bottom of the boat.

"Like what?"

"This," said Mickey, pushing a grinning

Chinook with his rubber-booted foot so the dog toppled off balance onto a fish. Mickey pointed vaguely around the cluttered and slimy scow.

"You mean dirty and gross?" Hank asked.

"I mean free and independent."

"Nobody's free and independent," Hank Hudson snapped. "Oh, for a little while mebbe it seems that way, but we live in these here bodies and in this here society, and we try not to give any danged numbers to any nosy bureaucrats, but they get 'em anyway and they make us be part of their idiotic system, at least part of the time, and . . ."

"What are you talking about, Hank?" Mickey interrupted. "I got lost back there."

"Life," said the old man, flipping a salmon over deftly. "I'm talkin' about life. We all start out your age thinking we know the answers the older folks can't seem to come up with, even though the answers are so danged obvious. Then we get old ourselves — like me — and, son-of-a-gun, we don't have any answers at all to speak of. Can't even remember the questions."

Mickey reached over the boat's side and washed fish slime off his hands in the bone-chilling sea. "And?" he asked.

"And what?"

"And what's wrong with just living like this? In the outdoors, like our ancestors?"

" 'Cuz our ancestors lived like this because they had to live like this — didn't know any different. Couldn't do any different. We do it for another reason entire."

"But the wilderness is real," insisted Mickey. "The rest is phony."

"No, Mickey-lad," said the old man, staring intently at the boy from beneath suddenly severe brows, his face wreathed in blue tobacco smoke from his furiously burning pipe. "For you —now—reality is town and school and the university next year, and the world. Take your strength from the wilderness, yeah. Teach your children to go to the woods and to the sea for their strength, too, sure."

Mickey looked searchingly at Hank Hudson, started to speak and then shrugged and went back to work, thinking hard while the old man smoked at the other end of the scow.

Mickey finally said, "You mean I have a job to do, huh?"

Hank Hudson did not seem to hear. He smoked and worked with the fish.

"Right?" insisted Mickey.

The old man threw down the last salmon, plunged his hands over the side and scrubbed, then shook the water off and rubbed his hands down a trouser leg.

"Right," said Hank Hudson. "The Lord don't like givin' brains to people and then havin' them people waste time foolin' around bein' selfish."

"Geez, you mean I'm selfish?"

"You been. You been, but then you're young, Mickey. Real young yet. You have a chance to make a bucketful of mistakes when you're young. But there comes a time . . ." He stuck his pipe between his teeth, stifling his own words.

"Hank?"

"Yep?"

"Were you?"

"What? Was old Hank what?"

"Selfish? A time-waster? You know."

"I been, a time or two," said the old man. He stared at the sea.

"Is that why you live out here by yourself, because you

were sort of screwed up or something?"

"Well, let's just say old Hank ain't lived up to his potential a time or two. But *you're* gonna," he said.

"You're the second person who has said something like that to me. You think you own me or something?" Mickey puffed himself up under his fish-slimy rain slicker, looking mock-angry.

"Yep," said Hank Hudson with a chuckle. "You saved this old man's life. Now we're blood brothers. As your brother, I'm a-tellin' you, you answer to old Hank."

"Editor says about the same thing, Hank. And he's every bit as mean and ornery and tough as you are. I've got real problems."

"Yep," said Hank Hudson. "You'll answer to Brother Hank and to the limey. Bless me, there's more than meets the eye with that one."

"He's a good friend," said Mickey.

"Yep."

"So are you, Hank. You're a real friend, too."

"That's a fact," said the old man. "That's a pure fact."

Hank Hudson pulled down the brim of his Stetson, installed his cold pipe upside down between his teeth and started the scow's big outboard. Soon they were scooting along in search of the cannery boat again. They were catching plenty of salmon and Hank Hudson's old wallet was beginning to fatten in his breast pocket beneath the plastic slicker.

To reach the cannery boat, they planned to run through Tlingit Pass, a dangerous two-mile stretch of water where tides raced at rapids-speed, and the water surface whirled and foamed. The scow, with its flat bottom and powerful motor, could carry them through safely. In fact, it was a thrilling ride, with swirling water as advertised. The boat bucked, dipped and jerked from side to side as it roared along, Hank Hudson bent down over his motor, his western hat tight on his head, his pipe thrust out like a pointer. The boy and the dog, both oblivious to any dangers, rode in the bow of the boat, heads up, taking the wild scene in with relish. Trees sped by close on either side, the tidal waters foamed and surged, and spray flew over the boat. Mickey was astounded as he watched the powerful current lash the rocky beaches and actually dash against the nearby timber.

The scow was soon through the pass. They found the cannery tender and began throwing their fish aboard. As they worked, the radio of the tender blared through an on-deck speaker: "*Cherokee*, this is *Jacky* . . . we got fish . . . and . . . soon . . . Tlingit Pass . . . ready . . . us." The message was broken by static but it was obvious that the fishing boat was trying the pass Hank and Mickey had just come through.

"Tell 'em to stay outta there," yelled Hank at the tender's open cabin door. "Tell 'em it's breakin' in the trees there. They better go around."

The message was quickly relayed.

"Already in," was the reply from *Jacky*.

"Tarnation," said Hank Hudson. "They ain't got the power on that old boat to keep her in the channel. Can't they read a blamed tide book? There's gonna be a shipwreck sure."

"Old Man Sipe's boat," said Mickey.

"I know," snapped the old man. "Him and that no-good kid of his. Well, let's go, then."

They hurriedly tossed up the last of their salmon, and without waiting for the count, roared off back toward the pass.

When they were half a mile in, pushing full throttle against the fierce current and making a headway of eight knots past the shore, an object appeared in the water ahead, grew rapidly in size, and flashed by.

"Jerry jug," Mickey yelled to the old man, who nodded.

Soon other objects, more jugs, a boat hook, a life jacket, swirled by the laboring scow in an ominous parade of colorful flotsam.

They eased around a final point of land and saw it. The fishing boat was broadside to the current, stranded on a rock. The *Jacky*'s mast was in the trees and she was laid over so her dirty bottom was almost fully exposed. The water pummeled her wooden hull, throwing geysers high into the air.

Hank Hudson ran the scow upstream from the wreck, angling in toward the shore, then turned the boat and ran toward the beach, picking up enormous speed before the scow crunched ashore and slid along the beach gravel, up and out of the water. It was a wrenching arrival. Chinook was thrown from the scow but landed running. Mickey and Hank Hudson were able to hold on and survived with nothing more serious than a good fright.

From the beach, where water thrashed by them at frightening speed, they got a clear view of the fishing boat not more than a hundred yards away. They could see Sipe and his son clinging to the rail of the *Jacky*, unable to help themselves beyond merely holding on. There was nowhere for them to go besides into the water, and that was out of the question. They would immediately be swept to their deaths in the maelstrom.

Hank Hudson and Mickey took a long coil of rope and some other items from the scow and cut quickly through the brush and timber, to come out on a rocky promontory that extended into the channel and upon whose far extreme the old fishing boat was stranded.

"Ever climb trees?" Hank Hudson asked Mickey.

"Some," replied the boy, following Hank's eyes upward and then out toward the fishing boat stranded on the rock. A lone old spruce clung to the shore, leaning slightly seaward. Some of its long boughs extended over the stranded vessel.

Mickey looked up at the tree and sighed. "Geez, Hank, I don't know." The extending limbs were at a dizzying height and the huge trunk of the old spruce was barren for the first twenty-five or thirty feet.

Hank Hudson deftly tied a hammer from the boat to the end of his length of rope, coiled most of the rope in a neat pile on the ground, took a portion in his hand, and told Mickey to stand back. The old man twirled the hammer around and around and let fly. The tool sailed into the sky in a true, curving ascent, up and over the limb the old man wanted. The rope, with the weight of the hammer pulling it, snaked down the other side.

"Perfect," Hank Hudson said. "Now all you gotta do is scamper on up there and drop them Sipes a line, Lad."

Mickey watched Hank Hudson tie a slipknot in the rope and pull the knot up until it was snug under the branch. The trapper put all his weight on it and it held.

"I'd climb it myself," said Hank Hudson, "but you know how it is when you get old." He winked at the boy, giving Mickey courage with his seeming unconcern over the feat the boy would have to perform to save the father and son out on the water.

Mickey stripped off his slicker, his wool jacket, his rubber boots and socks, and threw his wool cap on the ground. Without looking at Hank he grasped the rope and started up, bracing his feet on the tree trunk. He walked up the trunk and soon found himself sitting, frightened and uncertain, on a thick limb that extended away from him over the beach and then over the water far below.

Hank was motioning him outward, so he started, sitting on the limb and progressing with little bumpy jerks. Then he remembered the rope and had to reverse the process to get back, untie it and bring it along. He was certain he would fall, and it was a very long way down to where Hank Hudson's blurred face looked up at him.

Ten minutes after starting up the tree, Mickey was lying at the end of the limb, his aching legs wrapped tightly, one hand grasping the wood before him and the other swinging the rope end over the hull of the *Jacky*. He finally managed to drop it on the hull, and Sipe, inching along the rail, got it. After that it was simple. The Sipes tied their end of the rope to the rail of their boat, and Mickey, high above them, worked his way back along the limb to the tree. He looped his rope over the limb in a cross-over fashion so it wouldn't slip out the limb when he put his weight on it, and slid to the ground, shaking so hard he could barely stand. He and Hank Hudson pulled the rope down, securing it to the spruce, and the Sipes started slowly ashore, hand over hand. The fishing boat was rocking violently, though, threatening to slip from the rock and jerking the rope viciously. The father and son nearly fell off several times, but they held on like monkeys.

Tim Sipe was first ashore. His father followed close behind him.

"Nice," Tim said to Mickey when he came up the beach. "Not bad — for a Tlingit."

Mickey flushed in sudden anger and started to square off against the bigger boy.

Tim Sipe was smiling wanly, though, and holding his hands up. "Okay, okay," he said. "Just thanks."

Mickey nodded, "Okay," he said.

Tim's father came up. "Shake hands with Mickey," he said. "He saved your life."

Tim Sipe put his hand out tentatively and Mickey looked at it, shrugged and extended his own. They shook warily.

Tim Sipe finally backed off, heaved his heavy shoulders, hitched up his soaked jeans, tossed a shock of hair out of his shifty, dull eyes and said, "It ain't likely we'll ever be friends, Indian. . . ." The bigger boy was muttering from the side of his mouth. "But at least we don't have to be enemies."

"Right," said Mickey, "but there's one thing."

"What?"

"Don't call me Indian. Call me Mickey."

"Right," mumbled Tim Sipe, "Mickey."

ickey and Hank Hudson were in the float house, packing for the trip back to town.

"I hate to leave here," said Mickey, stuffing gear into his duffel bag and talking between teeth that clasped one of Hank Hudson's huge oatmeal cookies. The cookie was shedding crumbs and Chinook was busy at Mickey's elbow cleaning them up. The dog looked at the boy with pure love in his eyes.

"Can't get over that dog," said the old man. "He never took to anyone like he has to you, Mickey."

"Yeah," said the boy, and left packing to roughhouse with the animal. The boy and the growling dog tumbled about the cabin floor. Hank Hudson slapped his knee and egged them on.

Finally, the dog crawled away and lay panting.

"Hah," said Mickey. "The wolf dog quit. I guess I win."

"It beats all," said the trapper. "Ain't no one else except me could do that to Chinook and survive whole. By golly, boys and dogs sure do go together, now. Tell you what, Mickey — you can consider yourself Chinook's second master. You're in charge 'specially of making sure he's got his danged leash on when he's runnin' around town. Second master — deal?"

"Deal," replied the boy.

Mickey went back to his packing but stopped suddenly and looked in silence at Hank Hudson, who gazed back at the boy. "Been good to be here, Hank," said Mickey. "I learned so much."

"Been good for me, too," said Hank Hudson. "I learned some things myself."

"I'll always remember this place and you and Chinook — and that BEAR," said Mickey. "Geez, a lot has happened in a pretty short time. I'm feeling like part of the family, you know."

"Well," said Hank Hudson. "See, Mickey, it's this way. I figure I'm lucky you came along like you did — stowed away in my scow and all. I'm old, alone. Got a lot of friends, sure, but no sons. Never had a son. I'd like to sort of consider you . . . I mean, well . . ."

Mickey looked with a steady gaze into Hank Hudson's eyes. "Deal," the boy said.

"Deal," whispered the old man, turning away quickly to get his own travel gear together. "Get crackin'. We're a-goin' to see a glacier on our way back to town. Kind of finish up your wilderness education." The old man snorted. "Can't imagine it — a Tlingit who has never seen a glacier."

■ ■ ■

"Glaciers," said Hank Hudson, "are part of this land. They go way back before history, of course. They're mighty powerful and move where they want to move. About two hundred years ago, for instance, there wasn't a Glacier Bay a-tall, just glaciers and glaciers and glaciers right up to what is now the mouth of that bay. That's a historic fact. That explorer, Vancouver, he sailed by and saw it. Wrote it down. A century or so later John Muir, your naturalist, came and sailed way up into the place with those Natives in their canoe. The glaciers had moved back. They're still moving. They're alive."

They had worked the scow through floating ice ten miles up through the milky-green waters of a deep fjord. Now they were drifting near the face of a glacier. It loomed hundreds of feet over them, a colossal wall of blue, white and green ice. The glacier extended out behind the face in a great rising ribbon — a frozen, ancient river. It meandered up toward the far mountains until it finally disappeared from sight in a lonely high valley.

Gulls flashed across the glacier's face and waterfalls plunged down from the vertical rock walls that embraced the glacier on either side.

The ice creaked and groaned and snapped like rifle shots through the still afternoon. The sounds came from deep within the ice, but the glacier remained still, a sleeping giant wrapped in mystery.

Mickey whispered, "Hank, it's like we are in a church or something. Spooky."

Hank Hudson chuckled, pulled on his cold pipe, and stared at the sight. "Yep, well I know what you mean there, Mickey-boy. I surely do."

The glacier suddenly let out a cannon roar that shattered

the silence of the place, and then an immense curtain of cascading ice fell down its sheer face and plunged into the sea. The unleashed power of it was terrifying and Mickey watched openmouthed. Hank Hudson quickly worked an oar to get the scow bow-on to the wave he knew would follow. The seals on the nearby bergs ignored the commotion. Eagles continued soaring overhead. Gulls continued chattering. From beneath the glacier face where the ice curtain had disappeared in boiling frenzy, a wave began forming, moving toward the boat. The wave lifted icebergs gracefully before it, the seals riding their frozen rafts with unconcern. When the wave reached them, Hank's scow lifted in its turn and climbed the face of the wave, then descended the back side in a long slide and was still again.

"That was a little one," Hank Hudson said. "A big bunch of ice falls off, now, we pray the motor starts and we run for it."

"What are we doing up here?" asked Mickey, eyeing the glacier, looking for a hint that its entire face might suddenly fall.

"Lookin'," Hank Hudson replied. "Just lookin'. And thinkin'."

"Well, it's something to see, all right," said the boy. "It makes me feel sort of restful, except when that big piece fell off."

"Yeah," said the old man. "I figured you'd feel that way about a glacier. Stands to reason."

"It's like I've been here before. Like I belong here."

"Figured you'd feel like *that*, too. You know, there's something to that. You being Tlingit and all. Think how many Indians must have been here over the centuries. Probably camped right in this valley. Came up for the seals, don't you think?"

"Beats me," replied Mickey. "But, yes, it sounds reasonable. And maybe just to look, sometimes. It's a strong thing, a glacier. It's a thing to see."

They sat and stared and listened for most of an hour. Then the old man gave the outboard motor cord a yank, the engine roared to life, and they headed out of the bay. Mickey watched the ice recede astern. "I'll come back here," he thought. "I'll always come back to this place."

The visit had given the boy a sense of serenity he'd never felt before and he felt good about himself. He felt good about his friendship with the old man and about school, about town and about Tim Sipe and his kind.

"The glacier is magic," Mickey decided. "I don't even have to come to feel its power. I can just think about it and it'll make me stronger." Mickey waved at Hank Hudson across the boat and made a V sign with his fingers, holding his right hand high and waving it for Hank to see. "I just realized what you meant," he shouted to the old man over the motor's roar. "About the glacier — about everything."

"What?" Hank Hudson shouted, his words carried away by the wind and the motor sound.

"Never mind," yelled Mickey, waving a hand back and forth and grinning. "Never mind." He laughed, his young face wrinkling up, and Hank Hudson laughed with him, understanding it all.

Hank Hudson pulled his old hat down tight, stuck his cold pipe upside down between his front teeth, and they roared out of the bay and started across the strait for town.

21

Mickey Church strolled up from the harbor float alongside Hank Hudson. This Mickey was different from the one who had left town a few short weeks before. His muscles looked harder beneath his wool jacket. His face had lost all traces of its once-furtive cast and now was handsome and open. It was, all in all, an astounding transformation for the troublesome schoolboy. He was a schoolboy, and troublesome, no longer.

Editor had news. "Now, then, Laddie," the newspaperman said, sitting Mickey down at the familiar desk. "We have a barrel of forms for you to complete, so let's get to it."

While Mickey had been away, Editor labored hard in the boy's behalf. The acceptance to the university had arrived, but it was more or less a probationary one. With Editor's recommendation the registrar agreed Mickey could be admitted, but would be watched. He wasn't considered much of an academic achiever. His past record could not be erased by six months' hard work, or even a year's.

"But this lad has great potential, believe me," Editor assured the university official by telephone. "He is, I believe, the sort of Alaskan you'll ultimately be proud of."

So it was that Mickey gazed finally at his "Congratulations," accepting him as a freshman at the university. He ran his fingers over the words, and showed them to Editor again and again, until the newspaperman laughed.

"Lad," Editor told the boy, "you must go there and work and study and then you know what you must do when you have the requisite degrees in your hand?"

"Come back to Wrangell," said Mickey simply.

"Yes, I see it that way," replied Editor. "Learn, and then give what you have learned to others — to your town. You are a strong-minded young man, Mickey, strong in many ways. You could channel all that into helping others."

"You mean others who are bad kids like I was?" asked Mickey.

"You said it, Lad," replied Editor with a laugh. "But, yes. A lot of fine young people get off on the wrong slant and all too often there's no one who can get close enough to them to help them."

"Since I've been there, I can, you mean?"

"You weren't all the way there, thank God," said Editor. "But, yes, that's the idea.

"But you have to get through university first. Let's not get ahead of ourselves. Through university, and then the teaching degree — it *is* teaching, isn't it?" Mickey nodded. "I thought so."

Editor leaned close to the boy and said: "Temptations

you'll get up there, Mickey. You could slip easily back into your old ways with no one there to brace you up. Of course, if you do," he said, "you'll be answering to me, personally."

Mickey stared at Editor, then laughed quietly.

"There's a bit of the old temper remaining there," observed the newspaperman, grasping the boy's shoulder. "Good. Use that to your advantage. Use the enemy's strength against him." Editor made a certain sweeping body and hand motion so quickly that the unknowing would scarcely have seen it.

Mickey saw it. "I'll remember," he said to Editor.

■ ■ ■

When he opened the door to Blackie's and saw the checkerboard and the vacant chairs, Mickey felt an almost physical pain. He yearned for the grimy Louisianan and halfway expected Blackie to bang in from the shop in noisy greeting. Blackie's wife was there, smiling. "Long time, Mickey," she said.

"Yep," said the boy. "I miss him."

"Me too," said the woman. There was an awkward silence.

"Well," Mickey said finally, "how's the canoe?"

"Oh, fine. We been keeping the canoe wet with bay water. You want to see?"

Mickey was hit with the dank smell of wood and mold when he stepped into the dim, cool shop. The canoe loomed above him, filling the space more fully than the boy remembered.

"Wow," Mickey breathed. "I'd forgotten how beautiful it is. And how big. You think we can get it out the door okay?" He measured the opening at the back of the shop dubiously with his eye.

Blackie's wife looked into Mickey's face as if she were studying the color of his eyes. "Blackie said so," she said. "Wrote it all down. You want to read again what he wrote?"

"I'm sorry," the boy answered her. "If Blackie says it will go, then it will."

"Mmmm," replied the dark little woman, nodding solemnly. "The canoe will be born from this building. It will be like a birth. Blackie dies, the canoe is born."

Mickey was taken aback. "You compare Blackie to a canoe?" he asked.

Blackie's wife chuckled. "I compare my husband to what the canoe stands for," she said slowly. "Blackie was wise like a Native, Mickey — like us. He knew how important the canoe will be, that's why he wanted to build it."

Blackie's wife turned and went out through the greasy shop door to the office beyond, leaving Mickey alone.

22

aldo Bernet lived in a log cabin, something he had always dreamed of. When he had arrived in Wrangell, he holed up in the smaller and more tasty of the town's two hotels, but he felt cloistered. His room was musty from being almost perpetually closed against the rain, and it opened onto a cavernous, dark hallway with a line of cheap wooden doors exactly like his own, except for the plastic numbers. He had an old black-and-white television set, wired to the town's new cable system, but he seldom turned it on. What Bernet did with his spare time was get out his reference books and his papers, and work at his battered typewriter. He was painstakingly gathering data for a history of Wrangell. It was curious that no one ever seemed to have done that, despite a lavish supply of what Bernet considered exciting and compelling material.

For example, there was the time President

Warren G. Harding showed up in a warship and stepped ashore for a visit. Wrangell became modestly famous for a while, then the little town at the mouth of the Stikine River sank back to obscurity. There was a spectacular shipwreck when a cannery sailing ship, *Star of Bengal*, left Wrangell at the end of a packing season only to be blown ashore on Coronation Island, with great loss of life. Wrangell played a role in two gold rushes — the town's Wild West days — and drew such notorious characters as Soapy Smith to try their luck at fleecing the miners. There were plane crashes, bear attacks, confrontations with the Natives and many more major and minor events that kept the teacher's interest.

When Bernet ran low on material he could find in histories and magazines, he would visit *The Citizen* and pore through back issues. He would turn the yellowed pages of old editions, his face pressed close to the print, eyeglasses on the tip of his nose, and when he found something he'd exclaim: "Oh, my goodness," or "Well, well, well-well." And then Editor would be hooked and he would come over to see for himself what great wonder the gaunt professor had unearthed from under the newspaperman's nose.

Editor would read over Bernet's shoulder. "Mmmmm," he'd say, "that looks like a good one, Waldo. Mind if I use that?" Editor would always put it that way, and Bernet would always answer the same way:

"My goodness, it's *your* newspaper."

Editor would laugh and clap the professor on a bony shoulder and Bernet would wince and smile thinly, and press his nose closer to the old newspaper article, scribbling notes furiously.

It was Editor who told Bernet one day about the log

cabin, which became available when its owner moved Outside.

Bernet moved in. The place had a barrel stove that burned wood, oilcloth-covered kitchen table, real log walls, cedar shake roof, porch to sit on when he had the time — Bernet loved it. He moved his books and papers and typewriter in and set them up.

Between savoring his cabin in the woods, his history research, his teaching and just being in Wrangell, Bernet was the happiest of men.

The day Mickey went to the cabin to tell Bernet about the canoe, he hitched a ride out the road, then hiked the rutted trail through the forest and finally was banging on the heavy door and wiping his boots on the doormat.

Bernet pulled the door open, saw the visitor was his student, and smiled a welcome. "Teapot's on. Come in."

Bernet's eyes were bright. He liked visitors. Especially this one. He had watched the Native boy change before his eyes as the school year progressed, and he liked to think that he had had a hand in the transformation. The professor and Editor had had a few conferences about Mickey. Bernet, too, felt the boy had potential as a scholar and pressed Mickey in class to excel. He pushed Mickey to the point where he thought the boy might rebel. But he didn't. He just worked harder.

Mickey stirred lots of sugar into his tea. "I have something to tell you," he said.

Bernet sat down across the oilcloth. "Good news, I hope."

"Ah, sorta," said Mickey, watching the professor sip his tea. "See, we've built this big war canoe. It's a secret, but we want you to see it. We all voted and decided you should see it. Well, that is — I guess I insisted."

Mickey had planned his speech all the way out the highway, but when he said it, it got all jumbled and didn't come out at all the way he had composed it. He liked Bernet very much. Sure, he laughed with the other students at the teacher's excess of emotion when Bernet got excited about something in class. The teacher would rant and weave and duck and wave his long arms while explaining some particularly compelling bit of history. They all roared, including Bernet, the time he slipped and fell down, to disappear briefly behind his desk, as he was acting out a Wrangell scene.

"I get so excited about this," Bernet had explained, brushing himself off. "Don't you?" Nobody knew whether the fall was an act or not. It didn't matter. He was fun and he was exciting, and somehow he made them like work. It had been a successful year for Bernet, and for most of his students.

So Mickey had planned the speech to throw the entire picture before the teacher at once, to see the reaction. He waited for it now.

Bernet set his teacup down on the oilcloth. "Let me understand this," he said. "This is a real, full-sized dugout canoe? Can we say it is an authentic replica?"

"Yes," said Mickey. "It's authentic. Tom Lincoln was the boss. He made us do it right. And Blackie's wife. She knows a thing or two about canoes." He echoed Blackie.

"Wow," said Bernet. He'd never said that before. Mickey didn't know it was in the teacher's scholarly vocabulary. Bernet began walking around the little cabin. "Do you know the significance of this, Mickey? Of course you do. Does Editor know about this? He'd want a story. Oh my, yes. Tom Lincoln, you say. Fine chap. Who else? Blackie's wife. That means Blackie. Poor man. A loss to the town. He was rough-hewn but, oh yes,

I liked that man. Strong, strong character. Cajun — very different breed of American."

Bernet sat down suddenly and picked up his tea, then set it back down, jumped up and headed for his jacket and boots. Then he came back and sat down just as suddenly. "Finish your tea. When can I see it?"

So the tall professor, the newcomer to Wrangell, was in on the secret too as the Fourth of July launching drew near.

23

The night of the month's highest tide was, providentially, July 3, and it found the four of them — Tom Lincoln, Mickey, Editor and Blackie's wife — in the shop poring over Blackie's launching instructions and getting equipment ready.

Native paddlers had been let in on the secret and had seen the canoe, but the launching, they were told, was a private affair. They understood and did not press it, but the excitement among them was running high indeed. They would be ready bright and early next day to take their places in the canoe.

High tide at half an hour past midnight was the time the vessel would slip down the crude chute and first taste salt water. The four assembled the prefabricated parts of the chute, greased the slides from a five-gallon pot, and eased the canoe slowly back, click by painstaking click, with a come-along arrangement Blackie had rigged up for the purpose.

Finally the high stern of the canoe protruded from the tent at the back of the shop. The mud below shone in the moonlight. Water lapped ten yards away as it came nearer and nearer to the old building. It seemed to Mickey as if the ancient waters, which had not seen the likes of the canoe for decades, were coming to claim the high-ended vessel for their own. He told Blackie's wife what he was thinking.

"The water comes for it, yes. Blackie's spirit is with it, too. It is a night of importance," she said.

The tide came so fast at the end that its rippling, shiny advance could be measured easily with the eye. When the water lapped at the old building's pilings and began climbing them, the four went inside and by dim electric lights began the last-minute work. Inch by inch, foot by foot, the canoe moved toward the water. Finally it was eased back so far its stern extended over the bay ten feet above the surface. It was nerve-racking work. A slip and the canoe could be destroyed in a quick, heart-stopping, uncontrolled plunge.

As the canoe rose slowly it filled the building's cut-out rear doorway and Tom Lincoln knew they had committed the classic boatbuilder's bungle — put together a craft too large for the door of the work shed.

"It's going to hit the overhead there," he told his companions. "We've got a big problem, looks like."

Blackie's wife glared at him and walked over, bringing the instructions Blackie had prepared. She held them up before Tom Lincoln's eyes and pointed.

At that instant the canoe inched past the danger by an eyelash.

"I'm mistaken, you see," laughed Tom Lincoln, pushing

the worksheet down from his eyes, "it just cleared. Look at that."

"Mmmm," said Blackie's wife, folding her arms, the worksheet sticking out behind her back. "Mmmmmm."

Now the big canoe was out of the building, resting on an angle on the slide. All that held it from the sea were its restraining ropes. These were loosed inch by inch until the hull actually touched salt water. Then the ropes were cast off altogether and the canoe slid silently, smoothly into the moonlit bay.

"Bless me," breathed Editor. "That's a wondrous sight, to see a ship go in like that."

"It is born," said Blackie's wife. "It is born, Blackie," she said toward the sea.

Tom Lincoln wiped his brow with a rag and said, "Uncle would have smiled."

Mickey could not speak. He stared at the canoe riding high in Wrangell Harbor behind Blackie's shop. He thought back across the year just passed, and finally walked off alone along the shore, silently taking in the form of the dark ghost as it rolled gently on a passing swell.

Then Mickey took off his cap and threw it high into the night sky. He yelled "Ya-hoooo" so loudly that lights went on at the Totem Hotel nearby and perturbed voices demanded that the supposed partygoers pack it up and go on home.

But today was the Fourth of July. None of the launching party would be going home. There was much work yet to be done.

■ ■ ■

Editor had been right. It was a big story. Not just in Alaska, either.

Editor's own paper, *The Citizen*, played the story of the canoe's appearance at the Fourth of July celebration with a photograph that took up half the newspaper's front page and showed the canoe in full race in front of town. A long story accompanying it ran under this headline:

— BOY'S AUTHENTIC TLINGIT CANOE ELECTRIFIES 4TH —

A photograph of Mickey and Blackie's wife and Tom Lincoln, and a separate one of Blackie, ran on the front page, too.

The canoe had shot out from its hiding place behind the floatplane hangar near Blackie's garage at precisely noon, while half the town was still looking to sea after the finish of the annual tugboat races, which the smallest and raciest tug, *Rambler*, had won again.

Twenty paddlers manned the canoe. Ernie Gates, the building supply man, had agreed to play the role of the canoe commander and he rode in the high bow, his gray mane blowing in the wind, an authentic Tlingit robe thrown regally around his shoulders.

The speed of the big canoe was astounding and its appearance did electrify the crowd lining the shore. As it slid out of the bay and raced along the shoreline, a murmur rose from the crowd and there was much pointing and shouting: "Look at THAT. My goodness, where did it come from? Isn't it beautiful. A fantastic sight . . ."

Then a noise like an approaching train began to come from the depths of the crowd and soon it had risen and become a cheer. There was applause with the cheering. Some in the crowd simply put their hands to their faces, speechless, or shaded their eyes to be sure what they saw was real. For others there were outright tears.

Mickey saw it from the stern of the canoe, where he sat and watched the paddlers, bending and sweating, lined up in front of him. Tom Lincoln was a foremost paddler, his muscular logger's shoulders bare and brown and glistening as he counted a cadence and punched the water with his long-handled paddle.

Editor, who finally, after all his months of patient waiting, could break his canoe story, later dispatched stories and photographs to wire services, newspapers and magazines. All were published and Mickey was suddenly a famous boy. The last of his detractors dismissed their doubts, finally, about the once-troublesome schoolboy and allowed Mickey Church might amount to something after all. There were many congratulations and well-dones and Mickey's celebrity status lasted for days.

He was little changed by it, though. Both Editor and Hank Hudson made a point of warning the boy that if they saw him puffing up because of a canoe, which, after all, could never have been built without Blackie and Tom Lincoln and Blackie's wife and even Bill the gypo logger, why, they'd have to take a hand. Besides, Mickey wasn't so much interested in today as tomorrow. He had much to do, getting ready for five years of hard work at the university.

24

t was fall. The rains came down in earnest, flailing the face of the old high-school building.

Students, imprisoned inside, could barely see beyond the school's front lawn. Zimovia and Sumner straits were being whipped to a froth by a southeastern gale. Gusts of cold wind slammed homes, rattling panes in their aged casements.

In the history classroom on the second floor, class was about to begin. A Tlingit lad named Andrew Young was noisily chewing gum and casting sideways glances at the young, dark-skinned, well-dressed teacher.

Andrew whispered to a companion: "Watch what I do to this guy. He's new. He don't look too mellow." He gestured toward the teacher.

Jim Smith, the school's heavyweight wrestler, came up behind Andrew and put a big hand on the Native boy's shoulder, squeezing him. "No," the wrestler said. "You be a good boy."

Andrew looked up, questioning. "What? He special or something? He don't look too mellow to me," he repeated.

"Special," said the wrestler. "You've only been in town a few years, while this guy was up at the university. You never met him. Now you will. I'll give you a warning — don't push him." The wrestler laughed. "You'll lose."

"What's the big deal?" the younger boy asked. "He is a teacher, ain't he? He's the enemy. Fair game." He laughed a machine-gun-quick series of heh-heh-hehs.

The bigger boy clenched Andrew Young's shoulder tighter. "Cut it," he said.

"Okay, okay," the smaller boy wailed. "Ouch, cut that out!"

"You ever hear about the Native canoe and the Fourth of July here a few years ago?" asked the wrestler. "Got in all the newspapers. Even Outside. You must have heard of that."

"Something," replied Andrew Young. "I heard something about a big canoe coming out of nowhere and getting in the newspapers and on TV and radio and stuff. So what?"

"*He* built it," said the wrestler, gesturing toward the teacher, who was organizing papers, apparently unaware of the animated conversation going on a few yards away from him.

"Yeah?" said the Native boy.

"It's famous. So is he. He's okay. His canoe says something to me. And it should say something to you — especially *you*."

"Not to me," said Andrew. "I don't go for this history stuff. I like Corvettes and chicks and drinkin' and —" he patted his breast pocket, "smokin'."

The wrestler squeezed Andrew Young's shoulder so hard the young boy squealed.

The teacher put his papers down and looked, finally, at the boys. "Mr. Smith, do you feel combative today?" he asked.

"No, sir, Mr. Church, sir," answered the wrestler. "I was giving Andrew here a lesson in manners is all. He needs them bad."

The rest of the class laughed and so did the teacher. Even Andrew Young, rubbing his sore shoulder, laughed in spite of himself.

Mickey Church, the history teacher, ran a finger down his chart just as Dr. Bernet had done in this very classroom on a similar fall day that now seemed very long ago.

"Ah, Mr. Young, said Mickey, rubbing his hands together and looking straight across the room at the boy as if they were alone there together.

"Yeah?" said Andrew Young, raising a hand tentatively, then withdrawing it quickly to his side. "That's me."

"Do you like history, Andrew?"

"Naw," the boy answered, looking at his classmates, who did not laugh.

"I didn't either," said Mickey. "I probably liked it a lot less than you like it, Andrew. I was a better smoker than you are, too, I'll bet." The teacher stared intently at the bulge in Andrew's shirt pocket. "Probably a better drinker, too. But I quit 'em both — in time."

Andrew Young gazed at the teacher, who continued. "Ah, Mr. Young, you are Tlingit, are you not?"

Andrew Young colored and half rose from his seat. "Yeah, so what?" he said. "So what?"

"So am I," replied Mickey.

The boy was silent, staring across the space between them.

"Really, I am one," said the teacher. "In white man's clothes."

The class laughed and Mickey held up a hand, restraining them. "We'll get started now," he said.

"We're going to talk about Wrangell history. Oh, yes, there was lots of Wrangell history. We'll learn first about a Tlingit hero. His name was Towaatt, and he was *some* man."

Jim Smith raised his hand and Mickey nodded. "What about the canoe?" said the wrestler. "Are we going to talk about your canoe?"

Mickey Church straightened his tie, then loosened it, then gave up, pulled it off, and stuffed it into his jacket pocket.

"That canoe," the teacher said, his dark eyes sparkling. "Yes, of course; we're going to have a look at it — sit in it.

"Tell me, Andrew Young, have you ever sat down in a real Native canoe? No? It beats a Corvette."

The students laughed. They liked this tall, straight, well-dressed young man who commanded respect but at the same time seemed one of them — their generation.

"Really," said Mickey Church. "It's better than a Corvette. You can see a hundred, two hundred years into the past from that canoe. I know. So will you."

The young teacher looked out over the heads of his students through the streaked windows. Outside, the gale had eased for the moment and across the strait the looming form of Woronkofski Island began to emerge.

As he watched, the skies over the island opened up and a shaft of sunlight poured down on the high landform Mickey years ago had decided was Towaatt's personal domain.

It was a wild scene and it held the teacher spellbound. The island was bathed in a shaft of golden light at its upper reaches, but its beaches and the strait waters that lapped against them were gloomy and dismal and dark.

Mickey stared and thought he saw a small black form against the island's shoreline. It seemed to be moving. He imagined it to be a Tlingit canoe, traveling north to south, carrying Towaatt home through the storm.

The form moved in and out of shadows and grew dimmer as Mickey sent a thought-greeting across the strait to the old Native:

"I'm here, Towaatt. I'm where I promised I'd be, and I'll tell them about you — I'll tell them about *all* of you."

The canoe's form burst into a shaft of sunlight and plunged again as quickly into the mists. Finally it vanished in the eternal Southeastern Alaska rains.

APPENDIX

On Christmas Day and the day following in 1869, in Wrangell, Alaska, a series of violent incidents occurred between several resident Tlingit Natives and some members of the U.S. Army (then the War Department). The following are actual military reports filed by the army officers involved.

■ ■ ■

HEADQUARTERS FORT WRANGEL,
Wrangel Island. A.T., December 30, 1869.

CAPTAIN: I have the honor to submit the following report for the information of the major general commanding the department:

About ten minutes after 11 o'clock on the night of December 25, 1869, it was reported to me that one of the laundresses, Mrs. Jacob Muller, had been badly injured by a Stickine Indian, named Lowan, he having, while in her house, just outside of the Stockade, and in the act of shaking hands with her, bitten off the third finger of her right hand between the first and second joints, her husband, quartermaster sergeant, of this battery, and a citizen, named Campbell, being present at the time. Learning what had taken place, and that the Indian had escaped to the ranch, notwithstanding the efforts of the sergeant to arrest him, I immediately sent Lieutenant Loucks with a detachment of twenty men to take him, with instructions to bring him in, if possible, without bloodshed, and only to use their arms in case of resistance or in self-defense. Lieutenant Loucks immediately proceeded to execute the order given him, and returned, bringing with him the dead body of the Indian Lowan and his brother Estone, the latter being badly wounded in the arm, the cause of violent measures having been resorted to. The report of Lieutenant Loucks, herewith appended and marked A, will fully explain. Apprehending trouble, I had turned out the entire force under my command, and as soon as firing was heard at the ranch I immediately sent a detachment of ten men as far as the store of the post trader, some three hundred yards from the garrison, with instructions to act in concert with Lieutenant Loucks's party, should they require assistance. A picket guard was stationed around the camp, and everything placed in a condition of defense.

About 10 o'clock a.m. of the morning of December 26, 1869, the sergeant of the guard reported several shots in the direction of the store, and in a few minutes word was brought to me that Mr. Leon Smith, partner of the post trader, W.R. Lear, had been shot near the door of the store. Mr. Smith was soon after brought in to the garrison and taken to the hospital, where his wounds were examined by the surgeon, who pronounced them of a most serious character, fourteen shots having penetrated the body on the left side, just below the heart, and three in the left wrist. Nothing further occurred during the night, and at daylight in the morning I sent Lieutenant Loucks again to the ranch with a detachment under a flag of truce, with instructions to see the chief of the tribe, Shakes, and demand of him the murderer, the Indians to turn the man over to him there, or failing in that, I gave them until 12 o'clock that day to bring him in, notifying them that if at that hour the man Scutd-dor, whom I knew to be in the ranch, was not in my custody, I should open fire upon them from the garrison. I also directed Lieutenant Loucks to inform the principal chiefs of the tribe, Shakes, Torryat, Shonta, Hank, and Quamnanasty, that I wished to see and talk with them at the post as soon as practicable. This message I had sent to each of the chiefs by an Indian woman before Lieutenant Loucks left the post, and I am confident that it was delivered. For the result of Lieutenant Loucks's interview with Shakes and Torryat, I would respectfully call your attention to his report. On the return of Lieutenant Loucks to the post, and reporting to me the refusal of the chiefs to come to the garrison, their indisposition to deliver up the murderer, and the hostile disposition manifested by those present, all of whom were armed, I consulted with the officers present as to the propriety of carrying out my threat of firing on the village, and they were unanimous in the opinion that nothing but the most decided measures would insure the safety of the post. At 12 o'clock no signs were made of any disposition on the part of the Indians to comply with my orders; but their intentions to fight were made evident by the numerous persons engaged in carrying their goods to what they considered places of safety. I waited, however, without avail until nearly 2 o'clock, hoping that they might change their determination; and at 2 o'clock I opened with solid shot on the house in which I knew the murderer, Scutdor, resided; several shots struck the house, but the Indians maintained their position and returned the fire from the ranch, several of their shots striking in close proximity to the men. Later in the day fire was opened on the gun detachments from the hills in rear of and commanding the post, but fortunately without effect. This was replied to from the upper windows of the hospital, and, in connection with a few rounds of canister in that direction, soon drove them away. Firing was kept up on their part all of the afternoon, and a slow fire from the 6-pounder gun on the village was maintained until dark. The next morning, just at daybreak, they opened on the garrison from the ranch with musketry, which was immediately replied to, and seeing that they were determined not only to resist, but had become the assailants, I resolved to shell them, but having only solid shot for the 6-pounder, and the distance being too great for canister, I still continued the fire from that gun with shot and from the mountain howitzer with shell. The practice was excellent, considering that I have no breech sights for any of the guns at the post — notwithstanding that three requisitions had been made for the same — and after four shells had been fired, two bursting immediately in front of the houses, and two solid shots just through the house of the principal chief, Shakes, a flag of truce was seen approaching the post, and firing on my part ceased. The flag of truce bore a message from Shakes that he and the other chiefs wished to talk with me, and I replied that I would talk with them in the garrison; but that the murderer must be brought in, for without him "talk was useless."

Soon after the chiefs were seen coming over, and a party behind them with the murderer, who was easily recognized by his dress. Just as they were leaving the ranch a scuffle, evidently prearranged, took place, and the prisoner escaped and was seen making for the bush, no attempt to rearrest him being made. The chiefs on their arrival at the garrison were received by myself and the other officers, and a conference ensued. They were then informed that until "the murderer was brought in no terms would be extended to them; that on that basis alone I would treat." Finding me determined to have the man at all hazards, they then asked what time would be given, and stated that as a proof of their good intentions they would surrender to me the mother of the murderer. I informed them that they must, as they proposed, bring me the hostage at once, and in addition, the sub-chief of the tribe to which the murderer belonged, the head chief being absent up the Stikine River; and that, if the murderer himself was not in my possession by six o'clock the following evening, I would open on them and destroy the entire ranch, together with its occupants.

This closed the conference, and during the afternoon of the same day the woman and the sub-chief were brought in and placed in confinement. That evening, about nine o'clock, the murderer Scatdor was brought in by the chiefs and surrendered to me. The next morning, December 27, a court was organized by general post order No. 76, for the trial of the murderer, who was identified by the five chiefs of the tribe and by his own confession. For the proceedings of the trial I have the honor to call your attention to the accompanying report appended and marked B. In pursuance of the sentence of the court, the man was duly executed by hanging, at twelve o'clock and thirty minutes, on the 29th of December, 1869, in full view of the entire ranch, the five chiefs and the Indian doctor being in immediate attendance at the gallows. The execution passed off without accident, and the body remained hanging until sundown, when, by my permission, it was taken away by his friends.

Too much praise cannot be awarded to the officers and men of this command for their coolness and general good behavior, particularly when it is remembered that twenty-two of the men were new recruits, many of whom had never seen any service. I would particularly call the attention of the major general commanding the department to First Lieutenant. M. R. Loucks, Second Artillery, whose promptness and decision in carrying out the instructions given him entitle him to the greatest praise, particularly in his interview with the chiefs on his second visit to the ranch.

I would also call your attention to the report of Acting Assistant Surgeon H. M. Rick, United States Army, marked C, of the casualties which occurred during the trouble.

In conclusion, I can only say that, though regretting that extreme measures had to be resorted to, yet under the circumstances I consider nothing else would have accomplished the object in view that of bringing Mr. Smith's murderer to justice, and reducing the Indians to a state of subjection to the United States authority. Everything is now quiet, and I have no reason to anticipate any future trouble; yet my vigilance is not remitted, nor will it be, as I have no confidence in any promises made by Indians. They have shown their hostile feelings in this instance, and it is only through fear and the knowledge that any crime committed by them will meet with prompt punishment, that will keep them in proper subjection.

I would also request that the thirty-pound Parrot gun asked for in my last requisition may be sent to me at as early a date as practicable, for, had that gun been in position, I think two percussion shells would have brought the Indians to terms.

Mr. Smith died at eleven o'clock of the night of the 26th of December, 1869. His sufferings were terrible, and death must have been a relief.

Trusting that my action may meet with the approval of

the major general commanding this department,
I am, captain, very respectfully, your obedient servant,
W. BORROWE,
First Lieutenant Second Artillery.
Brevet Captain S. B. McINTYRE,
A.A.A. General, Department Alaska, Sitka, Alaska.
A true copy.
SAM'L B McINTIRE
First Lieut. Second Artillery, and Bvt. Capt. U.S.A., A.A.A.G.

■ ■ ■

A.
FORT WRANGEL, WRANGEL ISLAND, A.T.,
December 26, 1869
SIR: About 12 o'clock midnight, on the night of the 25th
December, 1869, it was reported through the garrison that the
wife of Quartermaster Sergeant Muller, Battery I, Second Artillery, had had her finger bitten off by an Indian. I proceeded to
her quarters to verify the report, and there saw that the third
finger of her right hand had been bitten or torn off by an Indian
named Si-wau, as all present stated. I returned for my saber and
belt, reported to the commanding officer, then set off for the
Indian village with a detachment of twenty men to arrest the
Indian Si-wau. Having arrived in that portion of the village
nearest to the garrison, I intended to enter Tow-ye-at's house,
expecting to find there the Indian I wanted.

Before entering Tow-ye-at's house, I met an Indian in a
red cap and shirt, named Scudt-doo,* who, upon being asked to

*This is the Indian who subsequently shot Mr. Smith.

do so, told me that Si-wau had left Tow-ye-at's house and gone to another near by, which he pointed out to me. I entered the house with twelve men, leaving the remainder to guard the entrance outside. Si-wau was sitting down near the fire opposite the entrance, with nothing on but pants. The position of the detachment in the house formed in single rank along the nearest side of the quadrangular space, with instructions to fire whenever I should give the signal. With Si-wau there were Esteen, his brother, Si-wau's kloodtchman, (wife,) and old Klootchman, (woman,) who was sitting up, and perhaps a few others sleeping in different parts of the house. I tapped Si-wau on the shoulder, saying that I wanted him to come with me. He arose from his sitting posture and said he would put on his vest; after that he wished to get his coat. Feeling convinced that this was merely to gain time, that he wished to trifle with me, I began to be more urgent. Si-wau appeared less and less inclined to come away with me, and in this, the latter part of the parley, he became impudent and menacing in raising his hands as if to strike me. I admonished him against such actions, and tried my utmost to avoid extreme measures in arresting him. About this time, Esteen, probably apprehending danger to his brother Si-wau, rushed forward in front of the detachment, extending his arms theatrically and exclaiming, as I supposed under the circumstances, "Shoot; kill me; I am not afraid." Si-wau seeing this, also rushed upon the detachment, endeavoring to snatch a musket away from one of the men on the right of the detachment. Still wishing to avoid loss of life if possible, I tried to give him two or three saber cuts over the head to stun without killing him.

In doing this I had given the preconcerted signal (by raising my hand) to fire. I should judge about six or eight shots were fired during the melee, and only ceasing by the Indian

Si-wau falling at the feet of the detachment dead. Esteen and the others running to their holes, everything became quiet. I then directed the detachment not to renew the firing until further orders. I had Esteen pulled out, and discovered he was bleeding profusely from a wound in his right arm near the shoulder. Two handkerchiefs were tied around his arm above the wound to check the bleeding. My first thought was to arrest him also, for interference, but afterward considering that he was intoxicated, and that his interference was to protect his brother Si-wau, who, in my opinion, was in the same condition of intoxication, I concluded that he had been sufficiently punished, and directed that he be carried over to the hospital for treatment, and that the dead Indian should be carried over to the guard-house.

While preparing to carry over the two Indians, a tumult of challenging by the guard outside the house, and Indians shouting to their friends, began. Leaving First Sergeant Dean to superintend preparations for the transportation of the Indians, I went outside and found there, near the door, the sub-chief Tow-ye-at, who, I suppose, did the shouting, and was the cause of the challenging. At that time I could not see whether Tow-ye-at was armed or not, although the men said he had a knife, and to beware of him. I told him (Tow-ye-at) that I had finished my business, and that I was about to return with the men. I told him that if he wished to say something to the soldier Ty-ee, he could do so in the morning. With that I gently led him toward the house and advised him to go to bed. That was the last I saw of Tow-ye-at that night.

The two Indians were accordingly brought over and the result reported to the commanding officer. I dismissed the detachment, and supposing no further disturbance would occur, was sitting in post surgeon's quarters, when, about an hour or thereabouts after my return, a shot was heard from the direction of the store of the post trader. Taking with me Private Magee I ran down there, and while on the way Private Magee drew my attention to an object lying on the ground near the plank walk running between the store and the garrison. Upon examination it proved to be Mr. Smith, the partner of William King Lear, the post trader. Mr. Smith was lying on his breast upon a low stump alongside of the plank walk, with arms extended and a revolving pistol fallen from the grasp of the right hand. I first supposed him dead, but by placing him in a more comfortable position and speaking to him, he groaned merely. I then sent to the garrison for a stretcher and men. At about this time Gleason and Henderson came up.

In order to preserve the body from attempted mutilation, the three present posted themselves near by to look out for Indians in ambush. After a few moments I went up in front of the store, and told those inside to bring out a blanket with which to carry Mr. Smith to the hospital. This done, I posted three men, who had been previously sent to defend the store, behind obstacles in front of it. After having remained posted with the pickets a short time in order to understand the condition of things around the store, and to observe any movements in the village, I returned to the garrison to inquire into the circumstances of the shooting of Mr. Smith, and to receive orders in the case. Directly after reveille, according to instructions, I proceeded with a detachment of twenty men under a flag of truce to the Indian village, to demand that the chiefs should come over to the garrison to settle the difficulty by giving up the murderer of Mr. Smith, at or before 12 o'clock m. that day; or, failing in this, that the commanding officer would open fire upon the Indian village at the expiration of the time allowed in which the surrender of the murderer was to have been made.

When within about a hundred yards of the village, my interpreter pointed out an Indian in a red coat as the one that the Indian chiefs were demanded to surrender. My instructions, and especially the flag of truce at the head of the detachment, as well as the lack of positive proof of identity, precluded any exercise of force to make any arrest this time, or to bring him down with a volley. I there met Tow-ye-at in his war paint and fighting costume, and communicated to him the demands of the commanding officer. Tow-ye-at refused both the interview and the surrender of the murderer. He stated twice that if fire was opened upon the village he would die in his house. I explained to them all that the commanding officer was not angry with all of them, only with the murderer of Mr. Smith, and that if the murderer was surrendered, friendship and good feeling would return; and still earnestly wishing and endeavoring to avoid the necessity of opening fire, I proposed even that the commanding officer might meet the chiefs half way between the garrison and the village, all parties to the interview without an armed escort. Tow-ye-at refused the demands and the modifications which I did assume to make in order to discover the least desire on their part to avoid trouble. Tow-ye-at was stiff. The members of his tribe were continually assembling, armed with Hudson's Bay muskets, iron spears, pistols, &c., and more than half surrounding me at different times during the interview, in their eagerness, and, judging from the aspect of affairs generally, evidently determined to have revenge for the killing of one and wounding of another Indian the night before. I insisted and repeated to Tow-ye-at that by having the interview everything could be satisfactorily arranged; but all to no purpose. After a talk of an hour or so with Tow-ye-at and his friends, including also

Mo-naw-is-ty, and many of his friends who were within hearing, Shakes at the head of his own tribe came over and took part in the interview. His manner as he approached was quite self-important. His friends, like Tow-ye-at, were, with few exceptions, armed with flint-lock muskets, with thumb and finger ready to cock their pieces and open fire in grand style. With Shakes' friends, added to those already on the grounds, about one-half of the bucks of the Stakeen tribe were assembled, I th——— Shakes of the demands of the commanding officer, but with no more success than with Tow-ye-at, with the addition, however, that if the commanding officer wished to see him, he (the commanding officer) could come over to the village to do so.

I told them all again that their village would be destroyed like the Kaik village last winter, and that wherever American steamers found them the same thing would be done again. I also made inquiries in reference to Corporal Northrop, Battery I, Second Artillery, who, it was supposed, had been in the village the night previous, and not been seen since that night. All said that he had gone; some said over to the garrison in a canoe, and others said he was drunk in the bushes.

I explained to them until I was tired of it, that the commanding officer only wished a friendly interview, and that it was but one Indian he wanted, the murderer of Mr. Smith.

Shakes indicated that he had no more to say, and believing myself that the whole matter had been fully explained to them all, nothing remained but to return to make my report of the result.

The Indians, so far from acceding to the demands in the beginning of the interview, became more and more stubborn as their numbers increased, and instead of facilitating a peaceful settlement of the difficulties, it seemed to me more probable they might have been increased by an accident even.

I consider that under the circumstances everything possible was done to effect a peaceful settlement, and nothing remained but to execute the threat attached or included in the demand.

Respectfully submitted.

M. R. LOUCKS,

First Lieut. Second Artillery, Officer of the Day

First Lieutenant W. BORROWE,

Second Artillery, Commanding.

A true copy.

SAM'L B. McINTIRE,

First Lieut. Second Artillery and Bvt. Capt. U.S.A., A.A.A.G.

■ ■ ■

B.

FORT WRANGEL, WRANGEL ISLAND, ALASKA.

December 28, 1869.

Proceedings of a trial of a Stakeen Indian, named Scutd-doo, at Fort Wrangel, Wrangel Island, Alaska, in accordance with the following order, viz:

HEADQUARTERS FORT WRANGEL,
WRANGEL ISLAND, A.T.,

December 27, 1869.

[General Orders No. 76.]

Prompt and decided action being absolutely necessary, the following-named officers and citizens will assemble at this post to-morrow, the 28th instant, at 12 o'clock m., for the trial of an Indian, named Scutd-doo, for the willful murder on the morning of December 26, 1869, of Leon Smith, a citizen of the

United States, at Wrangel Island, Alaska.

Detail: First Lieutenant Wm. Borrowe, Second artillery; First Lieutenant M. R. Loucks, Second artillery; Acting Assistant Surgeon H. M. Kirke U.S.A.; William K. Lear, post trader. First Lieutenant M. R. Loucks will act as recorder.

WM. BORROWE,
First Lieutenant Second Artillery, Commanding.

Present: All the officers and citizens named in the above order; also the following named Stakeen chiefs:

1. Shakes, Kah-ons-tay Hah Kotsk. 2. Ton-ye-at Hoots. 3. Shus-tah-ack Koun Kay. 4. Qu-naw-is-tay Kosh-keh. 5. Klah-keh.

Present: Scutd-doo, Wish-tah, the prisoner.

First Lieutenant Wm. Borrowe, Second Artillery, stated that the prisoner, on the night of the 27th December, 1869, confessed himself to be the Indian who murdered Mr. Leon Smith.

Each one of the above-mentioned chiefs identified the prisoner as the murderer of Mr. Leon Smith, the partner of the post trader at Fort Wrangel, Alaska Territory. Shakes, as well as all the other chiefs, upon being asked what punishment should be inflicted upon the prisoner for his crime, say they agree to whatever punishment that may be necessary. It is then announced that it is the will of the officers and citizens present during the trial that the prisoner, the Indian Scutd-doo, at midday December 29, 1869, shall be hanged by the neck until dead, in presence of the troops, citizens, and the five Stakeen chiefs, and that he should remain so hanging until nightfall, when his friends could remove the body. To which all the chiefs assented.

The prisoner, upon hearing this, replied, very well; that he had killed a tyhee, and not a common man; that he would see

Mr. Smith in the other world, and, as it were, explain to him how it all happened; that he did not intend to kill Mr. Leon Smith, particularly; had it been any one else it would have been all the same.

WM. BORROWE,
First Lieutenant Second Artillery, President.
M. R. LOUCKS,
First Lieutenant Second Artillery, Recorder.
H. M. KIRKE,
Acting Assistant Surgeon U.S.A., Member of Court.

The prisoner was then returned to the guard for confinement, till the hour of his execution, whereupon the trial closed.

WM. BORROWE,
First Lieutenant Second Artillery, President.
M. R. LOUCKS,
First Lieutenant Second Artillery, Recorder.
H. M. KIRKE,
Acting Assistant Surgeon U.S.A., Member of Court.

HEADQUARTERS FORT WRANGEL,
WRANGEL ISLAND, ALASKA TERRITORY,
December 28, 1869.
The foregoing proceedings are approved, and the sentence of the court will be carried into effect; the prisoner, Scutd-doo, will be executed at 12 o'clock m. of the 29th of December, 1869.

WM. BORROWE.
First Lieutenant Second Artillery, Commanding.

A true copy.

SAML. B. McINTIRE,

First Lieut. Second Artillery, and Bvt. Capt. U.S.A., A.A.A.G.

S. Ex. Doc. 67——2

■ ■ ■

C.

POST HOSPITAL, FORT WRANGEL,

WRANGEL ISLAND, ALASKA TERRITORY,

December 29, 1869.

SIR: I have the honor to report as the result of the late Indian trouble:

One (1) white man, Mr. Leon Smith, killed.

One (1) Indian killed.

One (1) white woman, company laundress, finger bitten off.

One (1) Indian severely wounded, by gun-shot fracture of the right humerus.

One (1) Indian hung.

I am, sir, very respectfully, your obedient servant,

H. M. KIRKE,

Acting Assistant Surgeon United States Army,

In charge of Post Hospital.

First Lieutenant WM. BORROWE,

Second United States Artillery, Commanding Post.

A true copy.

SAM'L B. McINTIRE,

First Lieutenant Second Artillery, and Brevet Captain U.S.A.,

Acting Assistant Adjutant General.